CW01618947

BLACK

Lew Grant

Ashgrove Crime

Ashgrove House Publishing Ltd
Office S4 Ashgrove House
Elland, Calderdale
West Yorkshire HX5 9JB

www.ashgrovehousepublishing.com

An Ashgrove House Publishing paperback

First published in the United Kingdom in 2011

All characters are fictitious and bear no resemblance to any person, alive or dead.

Paperback ISBN 978-1-908268-08-2

Printed and bound in Great Britain by
CPI Antony Rowe, Chippenham and Eastbourne

ONE

I was hit full in the face by a hard wall of heat.

The stewardess, looking fresh and bright even after the long journey, said goodbye to me with a smile and hoped I'd fly with their airline again. The standard formula.

Our eyes met and exchanged silent messages. It was unlikely we'd ever meet again but she had helped while away part of the twelve hour journey. For the first time, I had become a member of the mile high club. It was in the small hours. OK, it was in a toilet, and she was bending over the sink, taking it from behind, but it was better than the in-flight movie. It had not been the first time in a toilet for her. Nor, for that matter, for me. She had approached it with clinical efficiency, even to the point of placing a notice on the door telling passengers the toilet was out of order. A good-looking blonde - on her head at least – and while she had not been a memorable shag, she'd been better than a kick in the teeth.

Now, as I was leaving the plane, she smiled at me. I knew she flashed that smile for everyone – it was part of the training – but, I believed, she gave it that bit extra, just for me. She hadn't even asked my name. Probably had it on the passenger list. I hadn't needed to chat her up; she was the one who'd picked me out.

I'm always ready for a sexual encounter. What I was totally unprepared for was the heat. The wall of heat that struck me as I left the plane and walked down the steps to the tarmac. The day was hot, and it was only seven in the morning. I was glad to reach the air-conditioned terminal building and get my breath back.

I travel light: a small backpack and a suitcase on wheels that is easy to push. No problems at customs. And immigration was easier than I'd expected. The immigration officer, a pretty young black woman, looked at my passport and the immigration form

I'd completed.

'You were born in South Africa, Mr Grant?'

I nodded. I felt tired. I've always found it difficult to sleep in an upright position, and envy those who can.

'What made you leave South Africa, Mr Grant?'

'My mother took me to England. I was young. I'd no choice.'

'What's your destination now, Mr Grant?'

'Hopesfontein,' I said.

It was on the form I'd completed. Why do they always ask unnecessary questions, these people at airports?

'Where you were born, right?'

'Yes.'

She returned my passport, smiled, and wished me a good journey.

I took the train. That was my second mistake. The first, if you feel inclined to ask, was being born. I should have considered the bus but that would have been no better. I expected it would be pleasant travelling on a slow train across the high veldt, taking in the scenery. Pleasant? No way! It wasn't the Blue Train or the Shongololo Express; it was crowded, noisy, ill-ventilated and if it had been a horse it would long ago have been put out to pasture, or sent to the knacker's yard and made into glue. It stopped several times and not always at railway stations. Progress was slow, by any standards. I was in for seven hours of noise, sweat and loud music pouring out of ghetto blasters. Add to that, the fact that everybody on the train seemed to be talking into their cell phones, and in a variety of languages. South Africa has eleven official languages and about the only one I could not hear being spoken was English.

The view was not exciting. The city centre of high-rise buildings gave way to suburbs – upmarket housing alternating with shanty towns - and then to open grassland, with low shrubs and acacia trees. Gradually the vegetation became more sparse. These were areas of low rainfall.

Sleep was out of the question. I dare not stand up and walk down the train, for fear of losing my seat and my luggage. Many people were sitting on the floor in the corridors. The carriages were not exactly new. Seven hours without a seat would be too much to bear. At last, however, I needed to take a piss. When you gotta go, you gotta go!

The bog was not as clean as it ought to have been and the latch on the door was broken. Welcome to South Africa, welcome home, I thought.

On my return to the compartment, a woman was sitting in my place, as I'd feared. She looked old and tired; the skin hung loose on her brown wrinkled face. I shrugged, took hold of my luggage, and went back to walking along the corridor.

As I moved from one compartment to another, searching vainly for somewhere to sit, a girl coming the other way stood brazenly in front of me. She was an African but with a light complexion, and well stacked. Her red skirt was short and her white blouse almost covered generous and well-formed tits. In her right hand, inevitably, was a cell phone. She carried a small purse but no handbag.

'Hi!' she said, and flashed me a smile that was all white teeth.

'You travel light,' I said, pointing to the phone and purse.

'How far you going?' she asked.

'Hopesfontein,' I said. 'You?'

She shrugged her bare shoulders.

'Hopesfontein,' she smiled.

'What's a nice looking girl like you doing on a train like this?' I said.

It wasn't a question. It wasn't even an original remark, but striking up a conversation with a stranger requires an ice breaker.

'Looking for a handsome white guy like you.'

'For any particular purpose?'

'Sorry.'

'For what reason? Why?'

Hardly uplifting conversation, I thought, but I wasn't in the business of uplifting, and most conversation is banal anyway.

'Do I need a reason?' she asked.

'No.' I paused. 'What's your name?'

'Chiko. You?'

'Grant.'

'Don't you have a first name, Mr Grant?'

'Yes. But that's reserved for very few.'

'Like….who? Your mummy?'

I almost smiled. I liked her response. She made me sound like a snob *and* a mummy's boy.

'You don't sound like a South African,' Chiko said.

'Maybe that's because I'm English. But I was born here. In Hopesfontein.'

'Visiting relatives, are you?'

She was a nosy cow, I thought. Or just making conversation.

'I'm going to have a talk with my Dad.'

'He's still here? In Hopesfontein?'

'Last time my mother heard from him, he was. But that was nearly twenty years ago.'

The train moved at a snail's pace but every minute brought it closer to Hopesfontein.

I felt hungry and thirsty but there was no dining car and nobody pushing a trolley with drinks and crisps and sandwiches.

As well as learning the girl's name, I discovered she was aged in her mid-twenties – she didn't look it – had one kid, a daughter being looked after by her mother, was not married, but when she did it would be to a steady dependable white guy. I was white but many women in England would have sworn I wasn't dependable.

Most swear that I'm a complete bastard, fast with my fists, good with my dick, but certainly not to be depended on. We sat down together in the corridor and talked. If nothing else, the girl helped me endure the long slow journey and looking at her body had to be better than the unvarying veldt.

I walked out of the station at Hopesfontein and the first thing I saw was the baobab tree. Yes, I remembered that tree. Sometimes I had dreams in which there were people and scenes I had never encountered. That included the baobab tree. It's a strange looking tree, the baobab. The tree outside the station in Hopesfontein is old, large and gives shelter from the heat of the day for people and for motor cars.

'Now that's one fucking tree,' I said.

'I've seen bigger,' Chiko said.

'You have?'

'One hollow baobab in Zim is so large that up to forty people can shelter inside its trunk.'

'You've been to Zimbabwe?'

'I was born there,' she said.

There was a mass of taxis. No way could it be called a rank.

'You need a taxi?' Chiko asked.

I shook my head.

Memories were returning, clearer now.

'There's a hotel. In walking distance. I'm going there.'

'OK,' she said, and shrugged her bare shoulders in a way she did often. I wondered what she'd do when the cool of the evening came. I had a light jacket in my bag, and a long-sleeved woollen sweatshirt. She had fuck all.

'How well do you know the town, Chiko?'

'I've never visited this dorp before,' she said.

So that was it. She was going where I went.

I stopped, there on the street, outside a pharmacy, an *apteek*.

'I get it,' I said.

'Do you?'

I turned toward the shop entrance.

'I think I'd better top up on the French letters,' I said.

'Get a very good supply,' Chiko added, and she did not smile.

We passed a hotel called the Hopesfontein Palace Hotel. It belied its name. No way did it look like a palace. The exterior needed paint. The doors, peeling because of the harsh sun, cried out for varnish.

Hopesfontein centre was easily covered. The second time I passed the hotel I decided to go in and ask. I told Chiko to wait outside. Maybe when I came back, she'd have gone. And maybe not. Some tarts are like fucking limpets.

The young receptionist put down the romance she was reading.

'I'm looking for the Grant Hotel,' I said. 'I think it's somewhere -'

'This is it,' the girl said. 'This was the Grant Hotel.'

I was disappointed. I'd expected to see my name, and my father's, on a fine town centre hotel.

'How long's it been the Hopesfontein Palace?' I asked.

'About one year.'

'Mr Grant. He's still here?'

'No, Sir.'

The young receptionist looked serious.

'Do you know where he is?' I asked.

The receptionist looked troubled. She did not wish to answer.

'What's the problem?' A simple question. Do you know where Mr Grant is? Yes or no.'

'Yes,' she said.

'Yes…what?'

'I know where Mr Grant is,' she said.

'Then tell me,' I said.

'He…he is late.'

'Late?'

What the fuck was she talking about?

'Last year, Sir. Mr Grant….he took his own life.'

'He…..did what? Committed suicide?'

The girl winced. Like most of her people she could not bring herself to use certain words connected with death. Words like death itself.

'With a gun, Sir.'

There was in reception a small table with three chairs. The chairs were covered with red leather. Once, this had been a good hotel, allowing for the fact it was in a small high veldt dorp in the back of beyond. I sat down.

From behind a screen a man emerged. He was about five four, and fat, especially round his waist. He came over to me and sat down. We shook hands. Everyone did.

'Good afternoon, Sir. I am Elias Peteni. I am manager of the Hopesfontein Palace Hotel.'

The guy was proud of his position.

I did not speak. I was overcome with shock. I had expected that my father might be dead. After all, he had not contacted our family in England for almost twenty years. The shock was that he had taken his life by self and violent hand.

I was determined not to weep in front of other people. I was determined not to weep at all. My father deserved no tears.

'She said….your receptionist….'

'She is a good girl,' Elias Peteni said.

'She said that Mr Grant killed himself.'

'Yes. That is true.'

'With a gun.'

'Yes.'

'How? Do you know?'

Elias Peteni looked uncomfortable. Death was not something

to talk about. Evil forces brought death to people. Better not to talk about it.

'What kind of gun? How did he shoot himself?'

'I think you need to talk to the police captain, Sir,' Elias Peteni said. 'Me, I am new here.'

'Who owns this hotel? You?'

'Oh, no. It is part of a chain.'

'I see. This chain…..did they buy it before Mr Grant killed himself? Or after?'

'One year ago. When I became the manager.'

I stared at the reception area for a while. Did I remember it? Or did I think I did?

'Mr Peteni, I'd like a room.'

Elias Peteni smiled. Booking a room. This he preferred. Better than talk about guns and suicide. Booking a room, he understood. He went back behind the reception counter.

'Dorcas, a room for the gentleman. Single or double, Sir?'

I looked at the main entrance. Chiko was there still, talking to a taxi driver.

'Double. On the third floor,' I said. 'There's a special suite, I think.'

That was something dredged from memory.

'I give you the best room in the hotel,' Elias Peteni said, smiling broadly.

'What is the name?' Dorcas asked.

I took the back pack and found my passport.

'Grant. Lew Grant.'

That wiped the smile from Peteni's face.

TWO

I walked to Sol's house. On my back was my pack. I rarely went anywhere without it, and I wasn't going to leave it in the hotel suite. Certainly not with a woman I had only met that day resting in the room, watching TV.

In the late afternoon, with the sun sloping down, it was becoming cooler, more pleasant. There was a new building going up. A sign said that it was to be the new regional HQ for the ANC. A number of people must have done well out of the contract; that is how these things work, all along the line. Whether or not the Party needed a new place in a dorp like Hopesfontein hardly seemed relevant.

The house was a modest place with a small stoep right by the pavement. It was a run-down district. Probably always had been.

Sol was sitting on a rocking chair. He greeted me. He thought I was just passing by. Could tell I was from out of town. In Hopesfontein everybody knew everybody. Or just about.

'Mr Isaacs?'

Sol, who'd been prepared to greet the stranger, was now suspicious. A stranger who knew his name.

'Depends who's asking, son.'

'You are Sol Isaacs, aren't you?'

'Not if you're from Inland Revenue. Not if you're from the local party bosses. But you can't be: they all know me.' He looked deep into my eyes. 'Have we met before, son?'

'You were a friend of my father's.'

'You sound like an English boy to me,' Sol Isaacs said.

'I'm English. But my dad was a Litvak.'

That's all it took.

Sol Isaacs stood up, grasped my hand firmly, and pulled me

on to the stoep. He shouted into the house.

'Aggie! Two Castle.'

Another memory. Castle Lager, brewed by South Africa Breweries in cans with labels of distinctive red stripes.

Aggie was a small, old black woman with a wizened face. Was it the sun caused the lines and the sagging of the skin, I wondered. She put down the beers and went back inside the house. Said nothing to me or to Sol.

'What is your name?' he asked.

He must have been about seventy years old, although, like Aggie, he might have dried up in the sun, more prune than plum.

'Lew,' I said.

I rarely gave my first name but I wanted to keep the old guy guessing a little longer.

'What kind of name is that? It aint Litvak, for sure.

'My father gave it me. Or my mother,' I replied.

The old man's eyes narrowed.

'Here, you're not from NIA, are you?'

'NIA?'

'The new bloody name for BOSS. Bureau for State Security in the old days.'

'I told you, I'm from England.'

'Sure. A Litvak boy from England.'

'I'm not a boy,' I said.

Sol was almost squinting, as he tried to find in the corridors of memory the father of this confident English guy, this yiddisher kop, sitting on his stoep drinking his Castle lager.

'OK, I'll tell you,' I began.

'You tell me nothing!' Sol snapped. 'It'll come to me.' He paused and then rapped out, 'Alle menslike wesens word vry, met gelyke waardigheid en regte, gebore.'

'I'm sorry -'

'You're no South African,' Sol said. 'That's for sure. Or you'd have understood Afrikaans.'

'What were you saying?' I asked.

I'd picked up some of the language as a kid but had forgotten everything.

'All human beings are born free and equal in dignity and rights,' Sol translated. 'And here's some more: They are endowed with reason and conscience and should act towards one another in a spirit of brotherhood.'

'Sounds fine,' I said. 'Where's it from?'

'Article 1 of the Universal Declaration of Human Rights,' the old man replied. 'And I no longer believe anyone acts from reason and conscience.'

He sighed, looked defeated, but managed to summon enough energy to shout,

'Aggie! Two more Castles.'

Aggie emerged carrying a tray on which were sandwiches and biscuits.'

'And the beer?' Sol, asked.

'What did your last slave die from, Isaacs?' Aggie said, and went back inside.

Sol laughed.

'Gutte neshome,' he said. 'She's a good soul. Do you understand Yiddish?'

'Just a few words my mother sometimes uses,' I said.

'And your daddy?'

'I learned an hour ago that my father is dead,' I replied. 'One year ago.'

Sol Isaacs clapped his hands together. He stood up and shook me warmly by the hand, over and over again.

'David Grant's boy. You are…..'

Sol sat down again and I followed suit. There were tears flowing from the old man's eyes. I drank from my can of Castle lager and tried to look away.

Sol Isaacs took command of his emotions, wiped away the tears with a large coloured handkerchief, blew his nose, and cleared his throat.

'And how is your mother?' He paused briefly. 'Esther Hagar. David brought her out from the old country. Snaffled her from under the noses of the bloody Soviets.'

'She's alive and well, but can't get about as she used to,' I said.

I paused and drank more beer. I needed it.

'Was he a good man, my father?' I asked.

'He was a human being,' Sol replied.

'That isn't what I asked.'

'Human beings are flawed. Man is a dangerous animal. The most dangerous animal on the planet. Animals with machine guns. We slaughter our own kind. Good and evil? I don't believe in good and evil. They are social constructs.'

Sol Isaacs spat out on to the pavement.

'So what happened to reason and conscience and the universal declaration? Human rights and all that.'

'I quoted it. I never said I believed in it,' Sol replied. 'Bullshit, all of that. High-sounding, clever, but bullshit nevertheless.'

At that moment Aggie came out of the house on to the stoep.

'Watch your language, Isaacs,' she said sternly.

I smiled. Wondered why Sol Isaacs allowed his maid to talk to him like that.

'Come inside and eat, you men,' Aggie said.

She took the uneaten sandwiches and cakes.

I followed Sol inside.

We sat down at an old wooden table. Aggie had prepared dishes of salad and fruit. There was a jug of fruit juice and on a side table an array of beer cans.

'So,' Sol Isaacs said, 'you want to know about David.'

'Yes.'

'How much do you remember?'

'I…….I don't know,' I said. 'I was fourteen when we went to England. I can't say what I remember and what I have dreamed.'

'It happens.'

'Do you understand?'

Sol Isaacs took a banana and started to peel it, slowly, carefully. He seemed to be deep in thought.

I looked round the room. There were old photographs of Hopesfontein, and charcoal drawings, caricatures really, of men from the past: Charles Darwin, Friedrich Nietzsche, Giuseppe Garibaldi. I could tell who they were, because their names were writ large and clear under each drawing. There were others without names, which I didn't recognise. And then, to my surprise, caricatures of Karl Marx, Leon Trotsky and Vladimir Lenin. There were also book cases, stuffed full of books and pamphlets, and in pride of place along a ledge were books on communism and socialism.

'You are looking at the books,' Sol Isaacs said.

He had eaten his banana and had set to work on a bunch of grapes.

'Seems you're interested in politics,' I said.

'And you?'

'Women, money, movies.'

'Not politics?'

'No,' I said.

'I was always involved,' Sol said gravely. 'But not now. We expected great things when majority rule came, when Mandela was president – there is a great man – but the others…..well, as I said, they're human, with human failings.'

Sol Isaacs spoke quietly. Aggie was nowhere to be seen.

'We all expected more, better. We were stupid. Crime has been a major problem in South Africa since the end of apartheid. Assault, murder, rape. All on the increase. Crime affects society, you know. Many wealthier South Africans, black and white, have moved into gated communities. Too dangerous in the central business districts. More security in the suburbs, so long as you're behind strong gates and high walls. Selling razor wire. That's a thriving business. Worst in Jo'burg, but getting bad in other towns and cities.'

'Even in a dorp like Hopesfontein?' I asked.

Sol Isaacs snorted.

'I've been mugged twice this year. Me, an old man. Me, who worked for the cause. Went to prison for the cause.' He shrugged his shoulders expressively. 'Whatever they ask for, I give it to them. And they still beat me, the bastards.'

Outside, darkness was closing in fast. In South Africa there is almost equal day and night for most of the year.

'Many people have left. Crime is the main reason. And it's getting bad for commercial farmers. Only the other day Johannes Kaliesberg said he's packing it in and going to Australia. And Kaliesberg don't scare easy, I tell you.' Again, that expressive shrug. 'The busiest bloke in this town is Dr Molloi, the pathologist down at van Zyl.'

'Have you considered leaving, Mr Isaacs?'

Sol laughed derisively.

'Where shall I go, man? Lithuania?' He laughed. 'Israel? No way.'

I understood, or thought I did.

'Eat more food, my friend,' Sol continued. He paused, as if in meditation. I started to eat a sandwich.

Sol Isaacs explained how in the nineteenth and early twentieth centuries many Lithuanian Jews had settled in South Africa, refugees from the Russian czar. Others had travelled to

Britain or to the United States. The South African Litvaks had had a profound influence, in spite of their small numbers.

'Litvaks were the backbone of the SACP, the South African Communist Party. Writers. Artists. And Sol Kerzner became rich opening casinos in the homelands in the old days.'

I finished the sandwich and cleared my mouth with a glass of guava juice. Memories were flooding in on me of fruit enjoyed when I was a boy.

'Mr Isaacs,' I said. 'All this is interesting. I'd like to learn more.'

'Contact Marie van Niekerk at the municipal library. She knows the history. Of Hopesfontein. Of the province.'

'Thanks.' I paused. 'But you don't fool me, Mr Isaacs.'

Sol made as if to be angry at my rudeness. But the moment passed.

'You are avoiding the matter of my father,' I said.

'Yes, and I'm sorry.' He smiled. 'No fooling David Grant's boy, eh?'

'Why did my father take his own life?' I asked.

Sol raised his head and looked me full in the eyes.

'Who told you that?'

'The people at the hotel.'

'The bastards lie,' Sol Isaacs said angrily.

'So…..tell me.'

'He was murdered. It was made to look like suicide but your father was murdered.'

I turned away abruptly and went to sit on the stoep. But there were no chairs. Aggie had been busy in her quiet unobtrusive way.

I stared up at the sky. There was a large clear moon. I wanted to bay at the moon.

But I didn't want to weep. No tears from me, especially not for a man I had not seen for twenty years, and who had abandoned my mother.

Eventually, I went back inside.

'Mr Isaacs. Was he a member of the Communist Party, my father?'

'No.'

'Was my father an activist?'

'No.'

'Was he a supporter of *apartheid*?'

'No way.'

'Did he have enemies?'

'We all got enemies, son.'

'I don't……why would anyone want to kill me?'

'I tell you. People kill for fun these days.'

'Where did he die?'

'In his hotel.'

'Did he live there?'

'Most of the time. He had a house which sometimes he rented out.'

'Anyone in particular?'

Sol Isaacs looked serious.

'You don't want to know, son.'

I went close. I could smell the banana on his breath.

'I want to know, old man!' I said fiercely.

'Your father rented his place to whores.'

'Black women?' I asked.

'You got it right, kid. And that made enemies in all communities. White, black and Indian.'

'Who investigated? Which cop investigated?'

'Jack du Toit. It was an open and shut case, they said. So they gave it to Jack du Toit.'

'And where,' I asked, my voice low and dangerous, 'is this Jack du Toit right now?'

'Still in town, son. Hopesfontein. Except now he's a

superintendent.' Sol shook his head sadly. 'Let it rest, son. You can't bring your daddy back to life. Let it rest.'

'No, no! I can't.'

'You cannot change human nature, kid. Remember that. No matter what you do, no matter how hard you work and suffer for your actions, you cannot change basic human nature.'

'That's your life you're talking about, Mr Isaacs. I can change one thing.'

'What's that?'

'Find out who killed my father.'

'What then? Hand him over to the police? Or her. It could be a woman. And what will this police force do then? Slap his wrists and tell him to be a good boy or girl in future.'

Sol laughed in a hollow way.

I pointed my right index finger at the old man.

'I can find him and kill him. That's what I can do. Find him and kill him, with my bare fucking hands, if that's what it takes.'

Sol Isaacs placed his hand gently on my shoulder.

'I loved David Grant. He was my friend. My closest friend. Go out there, Lew, and find the killer.' He paused. 'Aggie,' he called.

Aggie came in from the other room. It was a small house; she must have heard everything.

'Telephone for a taxi, Aggie,' Sol said.

'I can walk. It isn't far.'

'And get mugged?' Aggie said. 'I telephone now.'

The tender look that Sol Isaacs gave her proved to I that this woman was not his servant.

THREE

The taxi driver refused to accept payment. I was surprised. The man said this was on the house: at his aunt's request. Aggie was his aunt. The driver produced a business card, dog eared, gave me his cell number – he referred to it as his cell number; as in cellular – and said to call him first whenever I needed a taxi.

On arrival at the penthouse suite, I knocked on the door. No answer. I persisted. Still no response. I listened carefully: no sound of a television playing. Chiko had either fallen into a deep sleep or buggered off somewhere.

I went down to reception and asked for a duplicate key, saying I had locked myself out. I started to climb the steps again. By now, my feet dragged. I had not slept properly for many hours, having left home early the previous day for Heathrow airport and the plane to Jo'burg.

On the first floor landing I heard the sound of music playing. I went to investigate. There was a small bar, crowded with mostly young men and women, all Africans as far as I could tell. There was a live band. Three young men – two white, one black – strumming guitars.. In the middle of the room, dancing alone, arms held in the air, eyes closed in what appeared to be pleasure or ecstasy, was Chiko. Her white blouse had slipped and showed most of her ample breasts. As she moved, the onlookers got a good sight of her nipples as well as her shapely legs. There probably wasn't a man in that room who didn't at that moment fancy shagging her. I was among them.

I toyed with the idea of buying a drink but remembered there were bottles in the penthouse suite, and in any case I was weary almost beyond the telling. I slipped away from the bar and resumed the weary trudge up the steps to the third floor. The hotel was the highest in Hopesfontein. My father had wanted the Afrikaners in town to know what a Litvak could do.

Back in the room, I opened the windows wide and switched off the air conditioning. One thing I hate is aircon during the night, no matter how hot it is. I noted that my room key, which was a card rather than a key, was in place on the writing table, and my clothing, the few items I had carried with me from England, had been placed in the wardrobe

I stripped to my boxer shorts, went to the bar, and mixed myself brandy and ginger ale. I lay on the bed, First, the drink; then a shower; and finally to sleep. And if the tart dancing down in the bar came to wake me, I'd tell her to fuck off.

I didn't even finish the drink. The next thing I knew I was being awakened from a confused dream by a loud knocking. I was covered only by a sheet. I threw this to one side. The night air was still and hot. I opened my eyes, which were sluggish. Ignore the knocking, and it would go away. Probably some silly bitch of a maid come to deliver a chocolate to my pillow. These things happen in hotels. Still the knocking, which was now an irritating rap-rap-rap, as if with finger nails rather than knuckles.

I went to the door and peeped through the security spy-hole. It was Chiko. I opened the door.

'What do you want?' I asked in a surly manner.

'I'm staying with you. Remember?'

She pushed past me and entered the room.

'I was fast asleep,' I complained.

'Me too. I am tired,' she said.

I went to lie down on the bed.

She went to the bar.

'Drink?' she asked.

I remembered my unfinished brandy and ginger ale, and declined.

She poured an orange juice for herself.

'I saw you dancing,' I said.

I was now coming awake. Feared that I wouldn't be able to get back to sleep easily.

'Was I good?' she asked.

'Your tits were hanging out, but your legs looked good.'

She smiled.

'I love dancing very much.'

'Even by yourself?'

'Especially by myself,' she said.

She sat on the edge of the bed. She stared at my boxer shorts.

'Our friend looks happy,' she said.

She leaned over and touched me.

I sighed. Goodbye to kip.

'Take a shower, Diweni,' I said.

'Chiko,' she corrected me.

'OK. Chiko. Get that sweat off your body.'

'Some men like sweat,' she said, and smiled again.

'Like Napoleon,' I said.

'Who?'

'Napoleon Bonaparte. Emperor of the French. When he was away at the wars, he used to write home to his wife Josephine and say he'd return in about three weeks and she wasn't to bath.'

Chiko puckered her nose.

'Why did he do that?'

'I don't know,' I said. 'As you say, some men are like that. It's called *nostalgie pour la boue*. A desire for the gutter, for dirt.'

'Are you like that?'

'Does it matter if I am?' I asked.

'No,' she said. She stood up. 'I need another juice.'

'Do you drink?' I asked her.

'I never take alcohol, if that's what you mean.'

'You don't smoke cigarettes. You don't drink alcohol. But

you shag like a rattlesnake. Right?'

She smiled. 'Right!'

'Run the shower,' I said, sitting up. 'I'll join you.'

Right there, in front of me, without waiting to go into the bathroom, she took off her blouse and her skirt. She was not wearing a bra but she had on a small thong. Too small for her generous, firm buttocks and child-bearing hips. She took off the thong and threw it down on the carpet. I

She bent down to pick up the items. I knew then that it might be some time before I went back to sleep.

FOUR

I was stopped at the entrance to the police compound by a man wearing the uniform of a private security firm. The guy did not look comfortable in his uniform. He was like something out of an old Viennese comic operetta.

I had never come across this before: a police service unable to protect itself or its compounds.

Eventually, after showing my passport to about six different people, I was shown into the admin section. I had to use the passport in place of the ID card everyone carried. Everybody asked me the nature of my business. Every time I said it was confidential, between me and Mr du Toit.

Finally, after about thirty wasted minutes, I was shown into the man's office. The officer dragged himself out of his comfortable chair, shook hands, and with a weary movement of his arm, invited me to sit down.

'Mr Grant. That's correct, isn't it?' du Toit said. He'd been briefed by subordinates. 'And you're from England.'

He spoke with a strong South African accent. I guessed his preferred language was Afrikaans.

'As you know very well from my passport,' I said.

'Ja, of course.'

'Every bugger wants to see my passport.'

'That's because you don't have the Hanis, Mr Grant.'

'Hanis? What's that?'

'Home Affairs National Identification System.'

'So now every South African has to carry a *dompas*,' I said, and immediately wondered why and how I knew that word.

'So you have spent time in this country,' du Toit said.

'Till I was fourteen,' I replied. 'What's a *dompas*?'

'You used the term, Mr Grant.'

'Yes, and I don't where it came from.'

Du Toit explained. He spoke slowly and deliberately, as if he were giving a lesson to a dim learner.

In the old days, the Pass Laws in South Africa were designed to segregate the population and were one of the dominant features of the country's apartheid system. A pass book without a valid entry allowed officials to arrest and imprison the bearer of the pass. These passes became the most despised symbols of apartheid. The resistance to the Pass Law led to many thousands of arrests and was the spark that ignited the Sharpeville massacre on 21 March 1960.

'So nothing much has changed, eh? In the new South Africa,' I said.

'It is a weapon in the fight against crime,' du Toit said.

'Yes, the fight against crime. That's why I've come to see you, Mr du Toit.'

'How can I help you?

'It's like this….'

'Would you like a drink?' du Toit interrupted. 'Tea. Coffee.'

'No, thanks.'

Du Toit took a pack of cigarettes from a drawer.

'Do you smoke, Mr Grant?'

I shook my head.

'Very wise. I try to stop but I fail.' Du Toit struck a match, lit his cigarette, and inhaled smoke. 'You were saying. The fight against crime.'

'Does the name Grant mean anything to you?'

Du Toit pretended to think, and then shook his head

'It is your name. Should it mean anything?'

'How long have you worked in Hopesfontein, du Toit?'

Du Toit bit into his lower lip.

'Three years. I'm coming up to my fourth year soon.'

'So you will remember the Grant Hotel.'

'Yes. Now trading as……you are a member of that family?'

'I am. My father built and owned that hotel.'

'Now owned by a national chain, isn't it,' du Toit said.

'You fucking know it is.'

'Why should I know that, Mr Grant?'

'I'll tell you why, Mynheer du Toit. Because as a police superintendent in this dorp, you make it your business to know just about everything that goes on. Who owns what. Who knows what. Who's shagging whom.'

'If by that outburst, you mean I am on top of my job, then I accept it as a compliment.'

'Twelve months ago,' I said – I was fed up with this man's pussyfooting around – 'you investigated the death of my father.'

'At the hotel. Ja. He killed himself.'

'I don't buy that,' I said.

'I can assure you…..'

'Let's suppose he did commit suicide,' I interrupted. 'How can you be sure? Was there a post mortem? Was the doctor a competent man?'

'Doctor Molloi is a most competent pathologist, I tell you.'

'This most competent pathologist. Is he still working in Hopesfontein?'

'At the hospital,' du Toit said. 'But I hope, Mr Grant, you do not intend to harass all those in this town who had some involvement with your father's suicide.'

'I intend to involve myself in anything that leads me to find out the truth about my father's death,' I said.

'Ag, yes. The truth.'

'Why do you sneer, du Toit?'

'There is something in the Bible, isn't there? What is truth, said Pilate, and then washed his hands of the matter.'

'I'm not washing my hands of any damn thing,' I spat out.

'I take it, Mr Grant, that you are not of our Christian faith,' du Toit said.

I shook my head. No matter how hard I tried to forget I was a Jew, there were a dozen goyim keen to remind me.

'I'm not of any faith,' I said. 'Yours or Tom Dick's.'

'But you care for the truth, you say.'

'No, I don't give a toss about truth in general. Just the truth about one particular death.'

'Your father's,' du Toit said wearily, and stubbed out the cigarette end.

'Which you investigated.'

'It was…when? A year ago?'

'Right. But you have records, I'm sure.'

'Why should I retain records of cases?' du Toit asked.

'Ah, so you admit it was a case.'

'In any matter of this kind, we have to rule out every possibility. Including homicide. And when everything has been ruled out, we can only conclude, with regret, that it was death by a person's own hand.' He paused. 'But whether we still have the records, or whether they are in Pretoria -'

'I'll tell you why you still have them, mynheer,' I said. 'One fucking very good reason. Since majority rule, since the restructuring of the police service -'

'Necessary,' du Toit cut in. 'It was structured like a military organisation. Military ranks. It was intended to fight insurrection. Now it is being reformed in order to fight crime in the land.'

'And crime rates have never been higher,' I said.

'Reform is not a simple process, Mr Grant. But….you were explaining why you are certain I have retained records.'

'Because,' I said, and I pointed my right index finger at the police officer on the other side of the desk, 'because, mister, in this new police force of yours, as a white man, and an Afrikaner, it is necessary for you to cover your arse at every turn. You're a police superintendent. You'd like to be a Chief

Super. But you're white. Oh yes, you keep records. And I'll wager they're not all in this office. Some are in notebooks at home. You've retained your position, Jack, because you're a crafty bastard, and nobody is going to shit all over you before pension day, if you can avoid it.'

'You should go into politics, Grant,' du Toit sneered.

He lit another cigarette. For a guy who wished he could give up, he was feeling the stress.

'So….let's see the records you kept of my father's case.'

'You'll need more than a demand, Grant.'

'I could see an attorney.'

'And what would he do, this attorney?' du Toit asked.

'Make a claim under the Freedom of Information Act,' I said.

Du Toit sat up straight. Now he was listening. I had hit lucky. I had guessed there was a Freedom of Information Act in the country.

'Promotion of Access to Information Act, 2001,' du Toit recited.

'That's the one,' I said.

'Then you, or your attorney,' du Toit smiled, like a cat up to its furred neck in the best cream, 'will know that there are at least thirteen grounds for refusal of access to records.'

I stood up.

'Well, that we must find out,' I said. 'Thank you for seeing me, Superintendent du Toit. I will be back. I'll make an appointment, and I'll bring a lawyer with me.'

'I don't think you'll find one in Hopesfontein willing to act in your behalf, Mr Grant.'

I smiled. Now it was my turn to lap the cream.

'Not from Hopesfontein. Some hot shot from Jo'burg.'

I walked to the door.

'Sit down, Grant,' du Toit ordered sharply.

I turned. Suppressed a sneer.

'Sit down. I'm sure we can conclude this to mutual satisfaction,' du Toit said.

The sharp edge to his voice had gone. He wanted to be conciliatory. That was an error. I was going to strike for the bastard's jugular.

'Bring in the records, Superintendent, and let's see what mutual benefit really means.'

Du Toit did not need to leave for the main office. He went into an anteroom. I followed. In this room was a large safe. Large enough to hold many records.

Du Toit turned and asked me to go back to my seat. He didn't want me to check the security number.

I went back to the office. There was a water dispenser. The kind that is purchased cheap, then costs a fortune in ancillary charges. I filled a plastic cup with cold water and drank.

Du Toit came back in with a file. It wasn't very thick. In it were papers and photographs.

'It was in the Grant Hotel, now renamed the Hopesfontein Palace Hotel,' du Toit recited, as though he were a witness in court. 'The shots were heard by hotel staff. They thought it was a truck back-firing.' Du Toit smiled briefly. 'They always say that. Remember, we live in a country where guns are heard regularly. Mr David Grant was found many hours later. He had shot himself.'

'Was there a note?' I asked quietly.

I'd had a glimpse of a photo and wasn't sure if I wanted to see more.

'No note. There is usually a note but not on this occasion.'

'Let me see the photos,' I said.

'Are you sure that is a good idea, Grant?' du Toit asked.

'It's probably a very bad idea,' I replied. 'I don't want to see, but I....I have to see. Do you understand?'

'Yes, Mr Grant, I understand. In your position....'

I went round the desk and stood behind du Toit.

There was a general picture of the room at the hotel, the suite in which I was presently staying with Chiko. Then a photo of a man with the top of his head blown off.

'It was a shotgun,' du Toit said.

I stared at the photo. I wanted to vomit.

'It was a 12-gauge pump,' du Toit said, clinically. 'The Swiss army knife of guns.'

I couldn't remember much about my father. If my mother had photos, she'd kept them hidden away. Now I had to see him like this.

I went to sit down. Du Toit got water from the dispenser. I drank deeply from the plastic cup.

'Let me see again,' I said, holding out my hand.

I studied the photos closely.

'I don't know about guns, du Toit,' I said at last. 'This is a pump action shotgun, you say.'

'Correct.' The word came out strong and clipped.

'That means,' I continued, 'you've got to pump it to get the spent cartridge out.'

'That's right.'

'You pump it and then you put the next one into the….'

'The firing chamber,' du Toit said.

'Yes, the firing chamber.' I looked at all the photos, closely. 'Pump one out and then put in the next one. Right?'

'Correct,' du Toit said.

He lit another cigarette. Looked at the wall clock. Soon be time to go home.

'And he – my father, my late father – he fired two shots. Right?'

'That is correct, Mr Grant.'

Strangely, I thought, the man in the photos, with his head blown off and his face no longer a face, was not my father. He was just dead meat.

I closed the file and gave it back to the cop.

'As I say, I know nothing about guns,' I said. 'But maybe you'd like to explain one thing.'

'Yis,' du Toit said.

'How come, my friend, that he blew the top of his head off and then managed to eject the cartridge and load for a second shot. Tell me, how did he manage that?'

FIVE

'What are your plans today?' I asked.

Chiko was not the easiest woman to rouse and I had to slap her bare arse to awaken her. Twice, And hard.

'What?'

'I'm going down for breakfast and then I'm going out,' I said.

She pulled a face.

'You don't like the idea of breakfast, do you?' I said.

'I never eat in the morning,' Chiko said, and she yawned.

'What do you do in the morning?'

'Sleep.'

'Then sleep, you idle tart,' I said.

I put the door key card in my shirt pocket and walked down the steps to the breakfast room. Which was also the luncheon and dinner room. This was Hopesfontein, and not some San Francisco, London or Johannesburg establishment.

I ate mealie porridge, and decided I preferred oats. I ate bacon and egg, with mushrooms, tomatoes, onions, and fried bread. I drank fruit juice and finished with coffee. Strong, no milk, no sugar. Enough to set me up for the whole day.

I sat drinking the coffee and reading the local rag. *The Hopesfontein Inquirer.* Adverts and local gossip. There was a column by Ezekiel Temba, which touched on national politics. People seemed to like Biblical names. I read the first two sentences of Temba's column and quickly turned the page. More ads for corn, tractors. In the WANTED ads, someone was seeking a hedge cutter, and I wondered how many responses they'd receive from guys who swore they'd always wanted to be a hedge cutter. There was a report of a chicken seminar, accompanied by a black and white photo of chickens. That made me smile briefly.

Outside, the sun was shining brightly, as it had done the day before and would do again the next day, right up until rain clouds gathered in the appointed season. Nobody here spoke about the weather. Because it was predictable.

Hopesfontein had another good point. It was so small a town that most places were within easy walking distance. I soon found the municipal library. It was in Jameson Street, just off the broad Mandela Avenue.

As I walked from the hotel to the library, I noticed that Hopesfontein had been constructed on the grid system, like many American cities, like Johannesburg itself. I noted First Street and Second Street, and a sign for a business in Sixth Street. Jameson was an exception.

A girl was sitting at a desk inside the lending section. She looked to be in her early twenties. She was not, I concluded, anything to write home about, and I'd have shagged her only in an emergency. An extreme emergency. On her table was a name plate. People here seemed to like those. Superintendent Jacques du Toit, otherwise known as Jack, had one placed prominently on his desk at police HQ.

'Miss Ngulube?' I asked.

'Yes, Sir. Where are your books?'

'Books?'

'The ones you are returning,' Miss Ngulube said.

'No, I'm not a member. I'm a visitor.'

'You may join for a short period,' she said.

'Very kind of you. But I'm looking for the librarian.'

'I am the librarian,' Miss Ngulube said, and I detected pride in her voice.

'So where is Mrs van Niekerk? I was told -'

'Mrs van Niekerk is no more with the library,' the girl said.

Sol Isaacs had told me Marie van Niekerk was the librarian and an authority on Hopesfontein, its people and its history.

'Do you know Mr Isaacs, Mr Solomon Isaacs?'

Miss Ngulube shook her head. Then she opened her computer and typed in the name, after I spelled it for her.

'I am sorry, Sir. This person is not a borrower.'

'Could you, Miss Ngulube, tell me where I can find Mrs van Niekerk?'

'She is living at Extension 7.'

'Is it far to walk?'

'It is far,' Miss Ngulube replied. 'And it is now too hot to walk. In the morning early, it is not too hot.'

I thanked her for assistance.

Outside the library two taxi cabs hovered. Had they heard there was a mzungu, a white guy from England, in town, walking in the hot sun with a pack on his back? Such a man must be in need of a taxi cab.

From my back pack I took my cell phone. I rang the number given me by Aggie's nephew. Within five minutes, he arrived.

'Extension 7,' I said.

'OK, boss.'

'What's your name?' I asked.

'Freddie.'

'I'm Grant.'

'Yes, everyone knows there's a Grant in town.'

'OK, Freddie. From now on, when I need a car, I'll phone you. Just keep the fares reasonable.'

Freddie grinned.

'Or you go to another driver.'

'No, I'll kick your arse first, and then go to another driver,' I said.

He smiled. His teeth were brown.

'Is it far to Extension 7, Freddie?'

'Ten minutes,' Freddie said.

He was a fast driver. There were signs indicating speed limits in kilometres, but Freddie ignored them.

We went into the suburbs. I saw a large sign indicating Extension 7. The houses were neat, set out in rows, and seemed, to judge from the gardens, to be of recent construction. Houses were not built for people, but for the convenience of the construction companies. Put down houses in neat rows and you saved on the cost of water and sewage pipes. Each house was detached: not like England, where there are terraced rows, and semi-detached houses. In Jo'burg there were high flats, duplexes, because of the shortage of affordable sites, no doubt. In Hopesfontein I'd so far seen only two apartment blocks, and neither was inviting.

'Do you have a number?' Freddie asked.

I shook my head.

'Mrs van Niekerk. Librarian in town. Or was. Do you know her?'

'I will ask,' Freddie replied.

This was a mixed area, black people and white, and several Coloureds, which is what in southern Africa those of mixed race are called. Not many white people, though, and usually not the very well off kind.

Eventually, after being patient, and using a mixture of languages, Freddie proudly announced that Mrs van Niekerk was to be found on Fifteenth street, number 47. Such was the layout of the grid, he found Fifteenth street very easily.

I knocked on the door. A face appeared at a curtained window. It was a woman's face, a white woman. She came to the door in her own good time. I imagined her straightening the scatter cushions on the sofa, arranging her hair a little, maybe reluctant to open to a stranger. And when she did open, the door was on a chain.

'Mrs van Niekerk?'

'Ja.'

'My name's Lew Grant. I'm a visitor in Hopesfontein. May I

talk to you?'

'You are talking to me now,' Mrs van Niekerk said. 'Wat is you naam?'

'Grant. Lew Grant. My father was David Grant.'

She slipped the chain. Now that I could see her full length, I noted that she was in her early fifties - maybe late forties – she was thin, her face unhappy, worried, and her skin apparently untouched by the sun.

'What do you want. Mr Grant?'

Like Superintendent du Toit, she had a strong accent. Her preferred language was Afrikaans.

'I want to learn about Hopesfontein. I was told you're an authority. *The* authority, in fact.'

'Who is telling you this?'

'Sol. Solomon Isaacs.'

'Ag! That old Jew. He talks too much.' Then she appeared to relax. 'Come in. I am making the tea now.'

I went back to the taxi and told Freddie to return when he received a call. Freddie said he would remain but there'd be waiting time. I told him to get back and find more fares. I'd call when I was ready, and settle the bill then. Freddie assured me there was no problem. I could settle before I returned to England.

I went back to the house. I knocked and went inside. Mrs van Niekerk had the kettle on.

'You drink tea?'

'Lots of it,' I said.

I noted that behind the door there was a coat rail. There was a long grey woman's coat, a mackintosh, and a wide brimmed woman's hat. No sign of a man in the house: no pipes, no smell of tobacco, no boots near the door.

'Do you like rooibos?'

'I can't say I know it,' I said.

'Please sit down Mr….Grant?'

'Lew Grant,' I said, 'David Grant was my father.'

'Rooibos is very good for the health, you understand,' Mrs van Niekerk said. 'Rooibos tea is harvested during the summer. That is our Summer, you understand. In the southern hemisphere. Most of the tea is picked manually. It is then bruised and cut. They use tobacco cutting machines. At this stage Rooibos is still green. Fermentation is essential in order to enhance the flavour of the tea.'

I heard the electric kettle switch off. Mrs van Niekerk went to the kitchen. I followed her. The kitchen was small, but functional. She poured water into the teapot. Just like my mother always did. She swore it enhanced the flavour of the leaves. It is true, and I do the same.

'You prepare tea like my mother,' I said. 'Did you know her?'

'What is her name?'

'Esther Grant. Was Esther Hagar.'

Mrs van Niekerk's brows knitted together.

'No, I do not…..you must understand, we attend the Nederlandse Hervormde Kerk. The Dutch Reformed Church.'

In other words, we are Calvinists, the elect, and do not mix with Protestants, Litvak Jews, or anyone else unless we have to do so strictly for business.

We went back to the front room and sat down opposite each other, divided by a coffee table on which there were place mats and a copy of the TV guide.

'Rooibos is fermented in mounds,' Mrs van Niekerk continued, anxious to be on a neutral subject. 'And then it is spread out to dry in the sunlight. Fermentation turns the tea red. Rooibos' nickname 'red bush' does not apply to a live plant since it is green until it is fermented. You understand. In the final process Rooibos is sterilized by steam, dried in commercial dryers, sifted and put into these packages.'

'You know a lot about tea, Mrs van Niekerk,' I said.

'You work in the municipal library for thirty years, you learn many things.'

'And now,' I said, 'you have retired.'

Her pale face was suddenly angry and became red, like the tea she had poured.

'I did not retire. I was made....redundant. Me! After thirty years of loyal service.'

'I met Miss Ngulube,' I said.

'Impressed, were you?'

It was not really a question at all. The voice suggested she detested the young woman, her successor, very much.

'Were you the victim of positive discrimination?' I asked.

'Positive discrimination is discrimination,' Mrs van Niekerk said.

She had not even touched her cup of tea.

'It is called The Employment Equity Act. Equity in the workplace, they call it.'

I understood. The aim was to promote and achieve equity in the workplace, by the positive advancement of people from designated groups identified as previously disadvantaged.

'It's a matter of quotas, is it?'

We all know what it is, Mr Grant. Taking jobs from we whites and giving them to blacks like Ngulube.'

'You don't think she's up to it?'

'That black pig?'

I was accustomed to plain language. This was going too far even for me. But I understood why Mrs van Niekerk should talk like this, such was her disappointment. I also guessed that she'd been anti-black even before majority rule, long before the Employment Equity Act.

'Black pig, Mrs van Niekerk?' I prompted softly.

'Wild pig. That's what ngulube means. Wild pig. And she is

black.'

Anti-black. Anti-Catholic. Anti everything that was not part of her Nederlandse Hervormde Kerk and its narrow Calvinism. Anti-Jew, certainly. No wonder my mother had left for England. What had made my father stay? And Sol Isaacs, that old Jew?

At last, Mrs van Niekerk got round to drinking her rooibos tea.

'I take it Mr van Niekerk is at work,' I said. 'Or perhaps….'

I had noticed she wore a wedding ring, though not an engagement band.

'I keep his name,' she said, savagely. 'For the sake of appearances, you understand.'

'You are divorced?'

'No, I bleddy refused him.'

I decided to change the subject.

'What made it worse,' she said, her mouth twisted in a way that made plain her bitterness, 'was that van Niekerk went north to Zambia. Of all the places. And took a black bitch with him.' She paused. 'It is called miscegenation. You know what that is? It is sexual relations across the colour line.'

'It used to be illegal in South Africa, didn't it?'

'It is wrong in the sight of God. A sin. You understand? A sin against God.'

I could not finish my tea. I stood up and said that I must leave. I'd taken too much of her valuable time already.

'You wanted to know about Hopesfontein,' she said.

'It will wait,' I replied.

At the door, I thanked her for the tea.

'I wouldn't mind,' Mrs van Niekerk said finally, 'but Miss Ngulube knows nothing about being a librarian. Doesn't even know what the Dewey Decimal System is. I ask you. Not even the Dewey Decimal system.'

I walked along the length of Fifteenth Street.

By the time Freddie arrived in the taxi cab, I needed a drink. Rooibos would not be enough to clean my mouth.

'Take me to a bar, Freddie,' I said.

'Bar? Or beer hall?'

'What the hell,' I said.

I didn't know the difference.

SIX

Freddie dropped me at the beer hall on the corner of Fourth and Mandela– refusing to take a beer himself.

There were many men in the hall. Some were playing pool, a game I had never liked. Others were talking quietly. As time passed, more men came in. There was a general air of unhappiness, which only alcohol would alleviate. In the afternoon, no women, not even tarts cadging free drinks.

A man came to sit with me. He had a Castle in his hand and was drinking from the bottle. I could see the wisdom of not giving out glasses to unemployed men with beer inside them. But a bottle can also alter a face radically.

'You OK, man?'

'Never been better.'

The man sat down.

'New in town?'

'Just visiting.'

'From the United States?'

'From England.'

'Pretty good that side, eh?'

'Good in what sense?'

'Work. A weekly wage.'

I did not argue. The grass is always greener…..

'Your first in Davy's?'

'What?'

I drank from my glass. Next time it would be from the bottle. Fit in with the surroundings, though my skin colour marked me out. All the other men were African or Coloured.

'Davy's Beerhall and Grill,' the man said. 'The name of this place.'

I had not noted the name when Freddie dropped me off.

'It's old, man. The oldest bar and grill in Hopesfontein.'

I looked at the floor, which needed sweeping, the pall of cigarette smoke, the green and yellow walls.

'It has an….a certain ambience,' I said.

'There used to be good food in here, man. Say, what's your name?'

'Lew.'

The man shook my hand.

'Walter. My friends call me PKK.'

'PKK?'

Yeah,' Walter laughed. 'You know, the James Bond gun.'

Different spelling, I thought, but what the hell.

'You like movies, Walter?'

'James Bond on TV, yeah.'

I finished my beer.

'Another Castle, Walter?'

As the time wore on, others came to sit with us. Everyone was friendly and generous. Soon, I had four bottles lined up.

I learned that Davy's used to have good food and foot-tapping live jazz.

'That tin roof vibrated, man,' Walter said.

'It was the only way a black guy got in here,' a man said. 'In the old days. As a member of a jazz trio.'

That evoked warm laughter, which in its turn led to orders for more beer. These guys might be unemployed but they had money for beer and cigarettes.

On one wall there were photos of jazzmen and of soccer teams. There were even press clippings, recording Davy's history as related in the local press. The soccer teams and players were from an earlier time. In England, no one put up posters of Kevin Keegan any more. Man United seemed to have a good following in Hopesfontein.

I learned that when the bar and grill first opened, way back in 1920, soldiers returning from wars in foreign parts, it had a double life as a bar and grill, and also as a shebeen. Out back, beer was sold to Africans barred from entering a *whites only* place.

'That bar is more than one hundred years old,' another man said.

The ancient scarred bar had seen a lot of service.

'It was rescued,' Walter said.

His voice was starting to slur but in that he was not alone.

'Rescued?' I asked, and for some reason that single word, or the way he said it, evoked a lot of laughter.

'From Braganza's.'

A Portuguese had opened a hotel in Hopesfontein. It was demolished after the owner's death and only the bar was rescued.

'Davy brought it here,' Walter said. 'In one piece.'

'You helped to carry it, PKK?' a man asked.

More laughter. More beers purchased.

'It wasn't always called Davy's,' someone said, but no one was able to remember its former name.

In the 1980s, as the nationalist government started to dismantle what they called petty apartheid, which was not petty to those on the receiving end, places like Davy's were open to all races. Which meant that whites stopped drinking there. A different ambience.

'Davy, he was a good guy,' Walter said.

Voices became subdued. Bottles were clinked in remembrance.

This is the kind of emotion I abhor.

'Who the fuck was this Davy?' I asked.

No laughter this time. No mockery of my English accent.

'Davy was a good guy,' Walter repeated.

'So why did he kill hisself?' a man asked.

'He.....he killed himself?' I said quietly, but audible to

everyone round his table.

'In his hotel,' Walter said. 'In his own room. With a shotgun. Poor bastard shot the top of his head right off.'

By this time I returned from being sick, darkness was starting to fall. Women were coming into the beer hall, young women mostly, in pairs, clearly looking for a pick up or free drinks.

One young woman entered alone. She was a looker. Enough to subdue conversation, enough to turn heads.

I sighed. The woman looked round, saw me. I wasn't difficult to spot: a bottle of milk in a sea of dark Castle.

She walked over to my table.

'Hi.'

I nodded but did not speak.

Her mini skirt was still short, her legs good, and the white blouse showed plenty of tit.

'I didn't expect to find you here,' she said, and she sat down.

The men crowded round: bees and a honey pot.

'I'm sure you didn't,' I said. 'What are you drinking? The usual?'

I walked to the bar, over one hundred years old, rescued from Braganza's by my late father. Chiko followed me.

'Coke,' I said.

'We got Pepsi,' the bartender said.

'Fine,' I said. 'In a glass,' I added.

The bartender poured the Pepsi into a plastic container.

'With ice?' he asked, looking at Chiko.

She shook her head .'No, with Bacardi.'

'No Bacardi,' I said.

'Sorry?' the bartender said.

'No rum.'

I paid for the Pepsi, didn't wait for change, and carried it back to the table.

Chiko followed sullenly behind.

'What happened to not smoking and not taking alcohol?' I asked.

Every man at the table was listening

Chiko shrugged her bare shoulders expressively.

She took a sip of the Pepsi.

'What are you doing?' I said.

'I.....you bought me a Pepsi.'

'Like fuck I did,' I said. 'That's my Pepsi.'

I took the drink away from her and started to drink it myself.

Chiko smiled, sat on my knee.

There wasn't a man round that table didn't wish it was his own knee.

I pushed her roughly to one side. Chiko sprawled on the floor. She sat there, looking puzzled.

'What have I done?' she asked, a good actress all the way.

'You fucking lied to me,' I said. 'No woman lies to me. Now fuck off.'

'But-'

'And I never want to see you again.'

Chiko picked herself up, brushed her skirt down with her hands, looked round, and then jauntily strolled, all eyes on her, to the door.

The men started to applaud, though whether for her exit or my strength, was not clear. Maybe a bit of both. They slapped me on the back.

'Fucking tart,' I said, and raised a newly opened Castle to my mouth. 'Cheers!'

I remained sober when others were getting merrier and more unsteady as the evening wore on. Walter also weathered the storm more successfully.

Eventually, we were left alone at a corner table. It was time to ask questions. I told Walter of my suspicions. I did not accept my father's death was suicide.

'I need help, Walter. I'll see you OK.'

'What do you mean?'

'Financially,' I said.

Walter treated me to a scathing look.

'I do not take money from a friend,' he said.

'Will you take another Castle then?'

Walter shook his head.

'Pepsi,' he replied.

'With or without Bacardi rum?'

'Without,' Walter said, laughing.

I ordered two soft drinks.

'Now tell me, Walter, about the people in Hopesfontein who'd like to see my father dead. Enough to kill, that is.'

'Many people,' Walter replied.

'Give me some names,' I said.

Back at the Hopesfontein Palace Hotel, having returned in Freddie's taxi cab – I needed to be careful; fares mount up quickly - I collected my key card from Dorcas, on duty at Reception and wearily climbed the steps up to the penthouse suite.

The day, I felt, had not been wasted after all, n spite of not learning much from Mrs van Niekerk. Walter seemed to have a good knowledge of the town and its people and I was pleased to have met him.

In the corridor, leaning against the wall, generous amounts of thigh showing, was Chiko.

I inserted the card and opened the door.

'Sorry,' Chiko said.

'I told you to go away, didn’t I?'

'I love you,' she said.

'Don't give me that shit,' I said. 'I don't believe in love, not that kind of love, at least.'

I went inside and closed the door. I needed to shower and sleep.

There was a tap on the door.

I opened the door.

'Please,' she said, 'I will do anything, anything.'

I looked at her, at the bare shoulders, at the shapely legs. Then I closed the door in her face.

I was soon in a deep sleep. Next morning, when I opened the door to go down for breakfast, Chiko was in the corridor, awake, leaning on the wall.

'Have a bath,' I said. 'I'll bring you some breakfast.'

'I don't eat breakfast,' she said. 'But I'll drink orange juice.'

'With or without Bacardi,' I asked.

After breakfast I returned to the room to find Chiko completely naked, fast asleep.

I considered shagging her there and then, without foreplay. I didn't consider long. I stripped off, straddled her, missionary style, and relieved myself. She woke up but only long enough to smile and hold me close. I wasn't using protection. I hoped she was.

I showered yet again, quickly, dressed in lightweight trousers and a blue shirt, and went down to Reception. There, I asked for directions to the hospital.

SEVEN

The sign needed paint.

This hospital was opened in 1947 by HE Gideon Brand van Zyl, Governor-General of the Union of South Africa, in the presence of His Majesty King George VI and Queen Elizabeth.

It was repeated in Afrikaans, where van Zyl became Gouwenour-Generaal van die Unie van Suid-Afrika.

I wasn't interested in van Zyl or the king and queen. I had come to see Dr Enoch Molloi, hospital pathologist.

Molloi's secretary was a middle-aged woman. She was reluctant to allow me access to her boss, especially as I had not made an appointment. I knew a jobsworth when I met one.

I explained that I had travelled all the way from England to Hopesfontein, especially to see the doctor, and it was important that he see me, as I had a plane to catch the next day. I've always found that lying comes easily.

The secretary went into an adjacent office. It had a glass door. I could make out her shape, talking to a man. When she returned, it was clear that she wanted to turn me away, but Molloi had agreed to see me.

'Do not stay a long time, Mr Grant. The doctor has to perform autopsies today.'

I went through to the doctor's office, and closed the door firmly behind me.

Molloi was aged about thirty-five and was of middle height. He was not wearing a jacket and a beer belly hung over his belt. He stood up and shook me by the hand.

'How may I help you?'

He checked his wrist watch.

I got the message.

'I have to perform autopsies. Two.'

'Then let me go straight to the point, Doctor. Last year my father was killed. I think you may have been involved in the post mortem exam.'

I had to give dates, names, circumstances.

'Yes, I remember that one,' Molloi said. 'I had just arrived in Hopesfontein from study in the States.'

'You took your medical degree in the United States?'

Establish contact. Be friendly. It paid off.

'Oh no,' Molloi replied. 'I went on a course. For a diploma. These days, in South Africa, people are impressed with qualifications.'

Molloi was happy to talk about himself and his achievements. He studied for a medical degree with the University of Natal (Durban), graduating MB, ChB in 1982. He did his internship at Umtata General Hospital and continued to work there as medical officer for three years.

'Then I was detained by the Boers. Three years. Solitary confinement. No books, no magazines.'

Very useful, I thought, when majority rule was established in the 90s after the release of Mandela.

'I completed my Master's in Health Policy in London.'

'And came to Hopesfontein one year ago, as Director of the van Zyl General Hospital,' I said. 'Congratulations.'

'It is a stepping stone,' Molloi said. 'Until I move to something more.......Ministry of Health, perhaps.'

'And you remember the post mortem on David Grant, killed with a pump action shot gun.'

'I assisted Dr Slabbert. He is now retired.'

'And living in Hopesfontein.'

Molloi showed the palms of his hand, upwards, to signify that he did not know where Dr Slabbert now was. And probably did not care.

'He retired three months after my arrival.'

'He was the Director of the hospital?'

'Yes, there was a period of overlapping. It was not an easy time for me.'

'Did you agree on your findings, Doctor? Regarding David Grant's death.'

'I have my notes somewhere.'

He looked up at the door. Called to his secretary. In vernacular. The woman entered, listened, went to a file, pulled out a report, gave it to Molloi.

He looked at it, reading swiftly.

'Death by gunshot wounds. Self-administered.' He closed the file. 'Open and shut case.'

'Do you know Superintendent du Toit?' I asked.

'Of course. How could I fail to know him?'

'He pointed out to me that there two shots. He blasted the top of his head off and then managed to eject the cartridge and load for a second shot. When I asked du Toit to tell me how he managed that…..'

'He could not do that,' Molloi said, and he opened the file again, reading more closely this time.

'Did you notice that when you performed the post mortem with Dr Slabbert?'

'Dr Slabbert sent me on an errand. He performed the autopsy himself.' Molloi said, neatly evading the question.

'It looks like murder to me, Doctor.'

'Then you must return and speak again to du Toit.'

I sighed. 'You have photographs there?'

'Yes,' Molloi said. 'But I do not think you should see them.'

'Why?'

'They are very painful.'

Molloi checked his wrist watch. He stood up. As far as he

was concerned, the interview was at an end.

'I have to perform two autopsies,' he said.

'You? Director of the hospital?'

'I am surrounded by fools,' Molloi replied, and his smile was a superior smile.

'Doctor Molloi.'

'Yes?'

'May I observe?'

'I already have a mortuary assistant.'

'Observe. Nothing else. I won't get under your feet.'

'Very well, let us to go the mortuary.'

The mortuary was in a small building at the back, where few patients and visitors could see it. It wouldn't do for the sick and dying to be reminded that this building could be the last one they'd be placed before burial.

Molloi changed into a gown and gave me one also. He covered his head with a cap.

The assistant had already placed a dead body on the slab. The body of an old man.

'Usually we do not examine the old. But this was an unexpected death,' Molloi said.

He had switched on a recording machine. Later, his secretary would type notes.

'African. Age seventy years,' Molloy intoned.

He started with a complete external examination of the body. The assistant gave him a scalpel. Molloi made a U-shaped incision from both shoulders. Skin and underlying tissues were removed to expose the rib cage and abdominal cavity.

'Are you OK?' Molloi asked me, and there was an amused smile on his lips.

'Never felt better,' I replied. 'How should I feel?'

Molloi continued with his task.

The mortuary assistant gave him a saw. Molloi cut away the bones of the rib cage, exposing the windpipe, heart and other chest organs. Next he cut free the intestines, liver, kidneys and bladder. This was not the cleanest part of the body. Luckily, there was little spillage of blood: the heart of a dead person does not beat. Thin slices were cut from each organ, for microscopic observation and for chemical tests.

Then Molloi made an incision in the back of the skull, cut round the scalp and lifted off the top of the skull. Very gently, he lifted the brain from the cranial vault, the protective bony box. All the time he was talking into the recorder.

'I do not remove the spinal cord. The brain and liver are retained for special examination, and then for research and teaching purposes.'

At the end of an autopsy, Molloi instructed the assistant to sew up the incisions.

'And now I wash my hands.' He opened a tap.

He switched off his recording machine.

'Performance of an autopsy does not interfere with an open casket funeral service. None of the incisions made are apparent after embalming and dressing of the body by the mortician.'

I nodded my understanding.

'The second one I will perform later,' he said to the assistant. And to me 'It is a child whose body was mutilated. You do not wish to see that.'

I agreed.

'I will walk to the gate with you,' Molloi said. 'After such work, fresh air is essential.'

'Tell me about Slabbert,' I said. 'Was he thorough, like you?'

'He was embittered. He was losing his post to…..to a jumped-up kaffir, as he saw it.'

'He didn't actually say that, did he?'

'In these matters, a man does not need to speak the words.'

'How do you rate his work, Dr Molloi?'

'You are very direct,' he said.

'I'm an Englishman.' I paused. 'So, was Slabbert a good doctor?'

'The hospital administration was generally good. Slabbert had his own people in place. They all knew each other. Had much in common. Now, under the new dispensation, people are given office for the wrong reasons.'

'Which…. wrong reasons?'

'Because of services to the Party.'

'The Employment Equity Act?' I said quietly.

Molloi agreed.

'Sure,' he said, ' I was detained. I was a party activist. But I also have my qualifications.'

'So, toward the end of his tenure, Dr. Slabbert was not as…..not as careful in his work?'

'I wouldn't say that,' Molloi replied. 'It depended on what kind of work he was doing.'

'Autopsies. Post mortem exams. What about those?'

'Blacks, Coloureds. His work was….perfunctory. He didn't care about such people.'

'Only whites,' Grant said.

'Not all whites, maybe.'

'What do you mean, Dr Molloi?'

We had almost reached the hospital's main gate.

'Which whites were not white enough for Dr Slabbert?'

'He was a narrow man in his religion,' Molloi said.

'He attended the Dutch Reformed Church?'

'The Much Deformed Church is what we call it,' and Molloi smiled.

I shook Molloi's hand.

'Dr Molloi, thank you. You've been very plain with me. I

appreciate that.'

'No problem,' Molloi said.

'I won't take up any more of your time.'

'That sign. The name,' Molloi said, 'that will have to go. But it is not easy. These are political matters. We must not alienate any group in our rainbow nation.'

'What about……..The Enoch Molloi General Hospital?'

Molloi laughed out loud at the suggestion.

'So long as it is not the Enoch Molloi Memorial Hospital,' he said, and he shook my hand again.' He paused. 'Where is your transport, my friend?'

'I walked.'

'Ag, you Englishmen. You do not fear the sun. And it is very bad for the skin.'

'Enoch,' I said, quietly. 'Did David Grant commit suicide?'

'No way,' he said, and repeated for emphasis. 'No way.'

I walked into the centre of the town. I found the railway station and rested in the shade of the large baobab tree. I wasn't sure if memories were returning to mind, or if I remembered what my mother had told me. It was a large tree: had seemed even larger when I was a boy. The spreading branches of the baobab looked like roots sticking up into the air, rather as if it had been planted upside-down. At night the white flowers opened.

I thought of my mother. It must have been tough when she'd left permanently for England, accompanied by a fourteen year old boy.

Across the square from the station front and the baobab tree was a supermarket. *Hopesfontein HyperMart*, the large sign stated. I went across. I expected to find loaded shelves, clear aisles, check outs, automatic scanning. But it wasn't like a supermarket back home. The aisles were obstructed in many places with sacks of mealie meal, flour made from maize. There had been some effort at organising shelves according to product, but that had broken down. Instead of check outs with time-saving scanners, there were two women only, both of Indian family origin. One of them – she must have been about twenty or thereabouts - was a stunner. I felt the hair on the back of my head stand erect.

I purchased chocolate. Went to the stunner. There were two people in front of me in the line. The girl dealt with one and then, to my dismay, was replaced by another Indian woman.

'OK, Zohra,' the relief said.

'I'll take a walk,' Zohra replied.

I paid for the chocolate and went to the main entrance. Zohra was enjoying her freedom in the sun.

I peeled the wrapper from the chocolate.

'Hey!' I said, 'this bar's almost white.'

Zohra flashed a wonderful smile.

'The sun,' she said. 'We can't help it. They become soft during the day, and hard again at night.'

'I know how they feel,' I said. Then added swiftly, 'Do you know the way to the Hopesfontein Palace Hotel?'

She looked at me. Her eyes were deep brown. I wanted to swim in those eyes.

'I'll show you,' she said. 'I need to walk.'

'Thanks. Zohra, isn't it? I heard your name.'

'Yes,' she smiled. 'And you're Mr Grant.'

'How…….'

'This is Hopesfontein,' she said. 'Everybody knows everything that happens.'

We soon reached the hotel. Out front, on the first floor, with steps from the road, was a lounge area. Behind was the dining room.

'I'll buy you a drink,' I said.

I expected her to cry off. Hopesfontein is a small town, everybody knows everything.

'I'd like that, Mr Grant.'

My heart lurched.

'Lew,' I said.

'I'll call you Mr Grant, if you don't mind.'

She went first up the steps. Her skirt came down to just below her knees. She wore neither stockings nor socks. Her calf muscles were strong and yet feminine.

On the lounge there was waiter service. I ordered two soft drinks.

'And now, Mr Grant,' Zohra said, 'tell me all about life in England.'

Across the other side, walking toward us, I could see Chiko. She did not have a happy face.

EIGHT

Chiko stared hard at Zohra. She spoke to her in a vernacular language. Zohra answered in the same tongue.

'Speak English,' I commanded.

Chiko's hands were on her hips.

'She says to keep away from her man,' Zohra said, her face flushed.

'I am not her man, and she's not my woman.'

'Don't you want me now?' Chiko asked, and her voice was that of a little girl seeking gifts from a doting father.

I stood up, pulled Chiko roughly to one side. I whispered in her ear. Looked hard into her eyes.

'Fuck off,' I said. 'Anywhere! Fuck off now.'

The waiter was watching. Taking it all in.

Chiko's eyes flashed defiance.

'Fuck off now,' I hissed. 'Or I break your fucking arm.'

I returned to the table. It was only large enough for two people.

'Mzungu shit,' Chiko shouted and then ran down the steps and away from the hotel.

'I'm sorry,' I said.

'No problem,' Zohra said, and smiled. 'I know these women well. They always want mzungus.'

Zohra's hair was black, and shone from brushing. Cosmetics had been applied lightly round her eyes. She was a dish.

'So you work at the *HyperMart*,' I said.

'My father is the owner,' she replied.

'Which explains why you could leave work. Just like that.'

'No. It was time for my break.'

'Why do you work, if your father's the owner?'

'Only family members get to touch money,' she smiled.

'Do you have to go back?'

'Of course,' Zohra said. 'But I have time off tomorrow.'

'What time?'

'All afternoon,' she said.

'We must meet,' I said, and I leaned over and placed my hand on top of her hand. She did not withdraw.

'I'd like that.'

'Right, you know this town. I'll leave it to you,' I said. 'I'll hire a car. You can show me the sights.'

'I'll bring the car,' Zohra smiled.

'And the sights?'

'I know a good place. You can be a tourist.'

'Here? One o'clock?'

'The post office,' Zohra said, 'at two o'clock.'

She stood up, smiled briefly, and walked down the steps, never looking back. She walked well – like a lady, not a tart.

That evening I was on cloud nine. Big mistake. Never allow emotions to cloud an issue. I had important work, finding out who, if anyone, had killed my father. But I like women, and Zohra was the best I'd seen in Hopesfontein, or hoped to see anywhere else.

I went down to dinner. I ate sparingly. The dining room was almost full and quite noisy. I went to the bar. No jazz group this evening, no dancing. And, I was pleased to see, no Chiko either.

Back in my third-floor room there were several TV channels to choose from, some in English. None appealed. I tried the radio: nothing there. I had no wish to learn the world news. I'd showered before going down to eat so I undressed and lay uncovered on the bed, staring at the ceiling, a pleased smile on my face. Then I remembered that it was in this room that my father had met his death. When I found the killer, I would kill him – if necessary, with my own are hands.

It was then that I started to consider buying a gun. I telephoned Freddie. Said I didn't want the taxi but where, in this dorp, could a man buy a small handgun, no questions asked. Freddie established what price I was willing to pay. I was surprised at how cheap it seemed. But then, it is not only in South Africa that life is cheap. Two hundred rand and you have the means to kill. Freddie said he'd call next day. I told him to come in the morning, if possible; I was going out of town in the afternoon.

I arrived at the Post Office exactly on time. It was a quiet time, siesta time for many people, in the heat of the afternoon.

Within minutes, I saw a Mercedes Benz approach. New S class, maroon. It purred to a halt. I wasted no time. In a dorp like Hopesfontein, there are many eyes, nothing is missed.

'Nice motor,' I said.

'A present from my father,' Zohra said.

'I take it you have more than one *HyperMart*.'

'Plenty,' she said. 'And a Merc dealership in Jo'burg.'

'Only one,' I said, teasing her.

'Only one in Jo'burg.'

The windows were tinted, to keep the sun out, and prying eyes, too.

'You father must love you,' I said.

'As if I were a son,' she said.

I made to open the window. She told me that was unnecessary: there was air conditioning.

'This is a classy car,' she said. 'Dynamic. With style. See the head and neck restraints.'

'You sound like a car salesman,' I said.

'Don't you like style?'

'I like your style,' I said. 'And I adore your lovely smile.'

The car had a good turn of speed and Zohra drove fast along a highway that was largely free of traffic. I was careful not to ask where we were going. Soon enough, I found out. There were signposts for a tourist complex.

About a mile away from the complex Zohra was stopped at a police road block. She said they were from Hopesfontein and were spending a few hours at the casino. A black constable greeted me in Afrikaans, and I answered in English. I felt self-conscious: the Vektor SP1, 9mm pistol was in my pocket. Freddie had assured me it was a good weapon, made in South Africa. There was no search. Whoever the police were checking, it wasn't a rich Indian girl in a classy Merc, accompanied by a white guy.

The complex was intended for tourists who wanted to take in something of the past with all the comforts of the present. It was a mix of grandeur and tackiness. There were ruins of old temples, ancient carvings, grottos. It was all an illusion, an idyllic ancient civilisation rediscovered. The African theme was dominant: life size elephants, cheetahs hunting, eland and springbok, wildebeest. No warthogs or jackals – nothing ugly, nothing to suggest that nature is red in tooth and claw. All swathed in an opulence that no ancient African city ever enjoyed.

Swimming pools, a golf course, entertainment centres, restaurants, diners, tennis and squash courts, hot air balloons - and then the central purpose of the complex: the slot machines and gaming tables.

'My father likes to come here,' Zohra said.

'He likes playing golf?'

'He likes golf, yes. And this is an excellent course. But he comes here to gamble.'

'Wasting the profits?' I asked, surprised.

'Getting money into the system,' Zohra replied.

It proved to be a VAT swindle. Cash sales that didn't go through the books. Funny money. No better place to get it into circulation than a casino. But I had only one interest. This beautiful young woman in her one-piece bathing suit stretched out beside the swimming pool.

'Are all Muslims in South Africa as open as you, Zohra?' I asked.

'Most of us. No nonsense about purdah. No yashmak. No burqa. We are not Arab peasants, you know.'

'Looking at you now, Zohra, I'm happy about that.'

Her breasts rose and fell rhythmically. I, dressed only in my under shorts, felt the strength of an erection. I leaned over and kissed her gently on the cheek. She smiled and closed her eyes. I repeated the kiss. Zohra opened her eyes.

'No,' she said.

'I wonder,' I said quietly.

'What?'

'Can we book a room by the hour?'

'I'm sure we can,' Zohra said. 'But we shall not.'

I did not ask the reason why. I was no spotty adolescent.

'My parents have already chosen my husband,' Zohra said.

She looked unhappy now.

'Have you met him?'

'Yes, twice.'

'And?'

'And what?'

'Do you love him?'

'I.....I may learn to love him,' she said.'

Tears started to roll down her brown smooth cheeks.

And then she added: 'And I must go to my husband a virgin. You do understand, don't you?'

'Shit!' I said, but I smiled as I said it, and the spell was broken.

After swimming, we walked round the grounds of the resort complex. Despite being in a dry land, the fairways and greens of the eighteen-hole golf course were in good condition. Sprinklers played in the early morning and late afternoon, when the sun was less hot.

We stopped near a baobab tree.

'The upside down tree,' Zohra said.

'It's an upside down world,' I said, taking hold of her hand.

She sighed. Ran her free hand along the tree's smooth bark.

'Adamsonia *digitata*,' Zohra said. 'I remember that from school.'

'Did you enjoy school?'

'It was the best part of my life. We were able to think. I loved English language and literature. I loved one teacher in particular.'

'A man?'

'Yes. From England.'

'And you loved him?'

'Yes,' she said.

'I'm jealous, Zohra.'

We kissed gently.

'He never kissed me,' she said. 'But I wanted him to.'

We walked on. She was leading me closer to the car park. Soon, it would be time to return to Hopesfontein.'

'The Bushmen tell a story,' Zohra said. 'God did not like the baobab tree which grew in Paradise. So he threw it out and over a wall and it landed on earth. Upside down. Yet it continued to grow.'

We had reached the Mercedes.

'At school, we read Shakespeare.'

'I know Shakespeare,' I said. We were in the car. 'Romeo and Juliet.'

'We didn't read that one,' Zohra said.

'Then let me tell you the story.'

'I know the story.'

'The new version,' I said. 'Once upon a time a handsome young Jew fell in love with a beautiful Muslim girl. He was English, she South African. It seemed like an impossible love.'

Zohra smiled.

'How did it end? They both died?'

'No way!' I said. 'She eloped with him to England and they lived happily ever after.'

On the journey back to Hopesfontein we hardly spoke.

She dropped me by the Post Office. We did not speak or kiss. The Mercedes slid away down the street, almost silently.

The sun was going down. I was tempted to go to Davy's for a beer or twelve. No, that was not the answer. Maybe there was no answer. This was a problem I needed to sleep on. That I had fallen deeply in love, I did not doubt.

Back at the Hopesfontein Palace Hotel, formerly the Grant Hotel, I collected my key card from Reception. Dorcas was on duty, and Elias Peteni, the manager, was still there. Both looked at me in a way I could not understand.

'Something wrong, Elias?' I asked.

'No…..no matata.'

I walked up the steps to the penthouse suite. The hotel was quiet, like a morgue. No music, no kids shouting. I liked that.

I opened the door. Once inside, I had the feeling someone had been in before me. I shook my head. Stupid! Of course someone had been in my room: the hotel staff to clean the carpet, place fresh towels in the bathroom, make up the bed.

I yawned. Forget about food, forget socialising. I was going to retire to bed and sleep. Maybe when I woke, I would know what to do next.

There was a knock on the door.

'Come in,' I called.

I expected a member of the hotel staff, who would have a pass key.

Another knock, louder this time.

I went to open the door. As I took off the latch, the door was pushed rudely open. Two uniformed cops entered. One carried a handgun. The other checked the bathroom, as if I might have an accomplice in there.

'What the hell's going on?' I said angrily.

Another man appeared at the door.

'Mr Grant, you are under arrest. I have to caution you -'

'Cut that fucking crap,' I interrupted. 'Under arrest for what, du Toit?'

'Serious offences,' du Toit said.

"Serious enough to warrant a police superintendent?'

'Ja!'

'Then spit it out, for fuck's sake.'

'Rape,' du Toit said.

I burst out laughing.

'Rape? I've never raped a woman in my life. Didn't need to.'

'And……sodomy,' du Toit said.

And turned to a constable. He nodded. The man snapped on handcuffs.

'Now wait a minute,' I said, no longer laughing. 'Which fucking liar has made …..'

I did not need to ask. Did not need to guess. A woman appeared at the door. A young woman.

'Chiko?' I asked. She looked different.

Chiko was not dressed as before, in a mini skirt that could double as a belt, and her shoulders were no longer bare, showing her tits. She wore a dark skirt down to her knees and her blouse was decorous. She was dressed as a schoolgirl.

'Is this the man?' du Toit asked.

'He is the one,' she answered, head down, demure.

'Chiko!' I said. 'You.....you lying little cunt.'

NINE

I was kept awake all night. In my cell there were no beds, no sheets, no blankets. I tried to curl up on the hard floor but every time a constable came in and woke me. By the small hours I was weary beyond words. It was then that I was taken out of the prison, bundled into a Land Rover or similar vehicle, and in the company of five cops driven out to a place outside of Hopesfontein.

I was given a shovel and told to dig. At first I refused. No way was I going to dig my own fucking grave. The cops – they looked more like hard men from a para-military force than members of the South Africa Police service – beat me hard with sjamboks. The sjambok is not plaited from thin leather strips, like ordinary belts. Instead, it is carved whole out of hippopotamus hide. My father, I remembered, carried one when out of town, as a defence against deadly snakes. Shopkeepers kept them under the counter as a means of deterring thieves.

One of the men who spoke good English gave all the orders. He informed me that when I'd dug deep enough, they were going to throw me in alive, and cover me with the earth and sand. I did not believe this but kept on digging: the whips were a powerful incentive. When I had sunk to my knees from fatigue, and could dig no more, the men lit cigarettes and pretended to ignore me. After resting, I started to dig again. Let these bastards know who they were dealing with. I was now asked several times if I was ready to sign a confession. Each time I replied with an oath, and each time was struck with the sjamboks. They could beat me till I died. No way did I rape that little tart, and no way did I stick it up her arse.

As dawn was beginning to break, I was thrown back into the vehicle. Someone remembered to collect the shovel. These guys had hardly endured a hard night's work. Money for old rope, for fuck's sake.

The drive back to the prison gave me a chance to close my eyes and sleep. When I was awakened – and in spite of the short duration, I felt much better - we were outside the prison gate. There was a large sign.

Judicial Inspectorate of Prisons.

Hopesfontein High Security Prison.

There was a box number. I didn't expect I'd be writing to the governor.

I was allowed to shower, with a warder keeping watch. No need for that: I had no intention of topping myself. Any more than my father would. My back and shoulders were covered with weals – and not the kind you put on motor cars or ox-wagons. The cold water from the shower stung me.

Then I was given mealie porridge to eat. I prefer oats porridge, but I was hungry. After that, in a police vehicle back to the police central office and to the office of Superintendent du Toit.

I sat down, gingerly, for the chair back caused pain to my whipped body.

'You are Lew Grant. Correct?' du Toit said.

'Yes.'

I'd decided already there was no point in playing silly buggers. Alienating du Toit still further served no purpose.

In front of du Toit on the desk were piles of papers.

'This one is a confession for you to sign,' du Toit said.

'And the other?'

'Papers from the immigration department, facilitating your removal from this country back to your country of origin.'

'With or without?' I asked.

'I do not understand,' du Toit said mildly.

'Charges. If I agree to leave quietly, will the charges remain?'

'They are serious charges.'

'They are false charges. What deal are you guys offering?'

'You are put on a plane. Tomorrow. That's the end of that. You become a prohibited immigrant for the future.'

'No more visits to the land of my birth?' I said.

'Correct.'

'No more contact with Hopesfontein.'

'No more nonsense about your father being murdered,' du Toit said.

'And if I refuse?'

'Seven years inside, my friend. At least.'

'Seven years. And I'll bet there's a lot of fucking sodomy inside.'

'You had better believe it, my friend.'

'Superintendent du Toit,' I said, coming over all formal. 'Let's get two things straight. I am not your friend. Not today. Not tomorrow. And second, you can stick your offer right where the sun don't shine.'

'An unwise decision,' du Toit sighed.

'Can I have water to drink?' Grant asked.

Du Toit indicated the cool water dispenser, and for me to help myself.

'South Africa's Constitutional Court has decriminalized sex between men in society,' du Toit said. 'But you forced this woman.'

'You don't really believe that, do you?' Grant said.

'That is not relevant,' du Toit replied. 'A serious complaint has been made.'

I sat down again.

'I don't want to sound like an American cop show, but…..I want to see an attorney.'

'You already got one. And bail has been posted.'

'On condition that….'

'What?'

'There's always a fucking condition, isn't there?'

'You promise to leave Hopesfontein. We transfer the case to Pretoria.'

'It won't stick, you know, this bloody stupid charge.'

'Maybe it will and maybe it will not,' du Toit said. 'If it fails, we get you for possession of a handgun without a proper licence.'

'Who paid my bail money?'

'It seems you have wealthy friends,' du Toit said, but explained no further.

'Seems some bastard wants me out of Hopesfontein,' I said bitterly.

I walked to the door. Du Toit rapped a command.

'Wag 'n oomblik, asseblief.'

'Come again.'

'Please wait a moment,' du Toit said.

'Yes?'

'You really should try to curse less, Mr Grant. There are warnings in the Good Book.'

'Tell me all about it next Sunday when we meet at the Nederlandse Hervormde Kerk'

'You will not be in Hopesfontein next Sunday, Mr Grant.'

'Oh, no,' I said, and smiled. 'I'd forgotten that.'

Outside there was a car and a driver. The car was a new Mercedes-Benz Vito CrewBus. The driver was an African in chauffeur's uniform, complete with cap.

I shook the man's hand.

'Nice motor,' I said. I was being polite. I've no interest in car talk. Or even car torque, for that matter.

Top of the range,' the driver replied. She can carry up to eight people in comfort.'

'I climbed in and sat beside the driver.

'Designed for comfortable long-distance motoring,' the driver said. 'The seats can be attached to mounting points with quick-release locks. This helps make it easy for removing the seats and adapting the interior. All seats, as you see, Sir, are fitted with integral three-point seat belts, and head restraints.'

'You've been reading the sales brochure,' I said.

The driver laughed.

'So.......who owns this top-of-the range lump of metal?'

'Kaspar Molodi,' the diver replied.

'I'm new in town,' Grant said. 'Tell me, who is Mr Kaspar Molodi?

The driver's eyes opened wide.

'Ag, you do not know Kaspar?'

'No, I don't. So….. suppose you tell me who he is and where the fuck you are taking me. If it's Jo'burg, I get out here and walk back.'

'Not Jo'burg, Sir. I am taking you to Kaspar's house..'

'Nice house, is it?'

'It is very large, Sir.'

'And your boss, the mysterious Mr Kaspar Molodi. Is he a good employer?'

The driver did not answer. Maybe he thought the Merc was bugged.

By now we had left the metalled road and were on a graded laterite road. A good surface, but lots of dust thrown up behind the car.

'Stop this vehicle,' I said, in a stern voice.

The driver obeyed.

'You want to relieve yourself, Sir?'

'No, ' I said, 'I haven't drunk enough to want a piss. But enough's enough! Tell your Mr Molodi -'

The driver looked scared. 'No, Sir, please, I am asking you. My job….'

'He'll fire you?' I asked.

'I have a wife and five kids.'

'You should keep your prick in your pocket,' I said.

The driver indicated the door of the Merc.

'So, tell me. What's the secret? Who is Kaspar Molodi?'

TEN

Molodi's place was set on a hilltop, about twenty-five miles from Hopesfontein, overlooking the plain below. From a distance it looked like a hotel complex. There were high walls all round, with glass and razor wire on top of the walls.

At the main gate – the only gate I could detect – there were armed guards, dressed in uniforms that are usual for private security companies. I was not surprised to see they wore dark glasses, tonton macoute style, US traffic cop style, protect the eyes from the sun style. Intimidate anyone who needed to be fucking intimidated style.

The driver stopped at the gate. A white guy nodded to me, and then peered into the Merc. He signalled for me to get out. I obeyed. I was frisked.

'Grant?' the man asked.

'So you're expecting me,' I said.

'Atah Mevin Ivrit?' the guard said.

'That doesn't sound like Afrikaans,' I said.

'Atah Tzodek,' the man replied. 'You are right, my friend.'

He smiled. I decided not to indulge him with questions. Nor did I smile.

The gate was operated electronically.

'Come with me,' the white guard said.

'I'd prefer a pretty girl,' I said.

The driver started up the engine again and drove off to the right and behind the house.

'Well, the tradesman's entrance this aint,' I said.

Inside, patrolling with large dogs, were black and white security men. The grass was very green, had clearly been watered every day, and kept closely cropped.

There was a pool at the front of the house, with water lilies floating. I stopped to examine the flowers. I knew nothing about water lilies. I was making a point. I was a guest, not a prisoner. That's what I hoped, anyway. The lilies had delicate white flowers with yellow centres.

The guard stopped at the entrance to the house. It wasn't a door, but another gate, black, strong. The guard at this door, also attired in security uniform, like some guy from a Viennese operetta - was there a guard on the shit house door, I wondered – was also white, but there the resemblance to operetta ended. He had muscular brown arms and cradled a Uzi. As in small lightweight sub-machine gun.

The two guards spoke together, and they laughed. I did not react. Didn't understand a single word.

One guy removed his shades, Retro designer shades, must have cost a fortune, but maybe Mr Molodi paid the bill.

'Grant is the name, isn't it?'

'Sure.'

'So what kind of guy with a name like Grant doesn't understand any Hebrew?'

'The kind of guy with a name like Grant who comes from England and never attends synagogue. That kind of guy. Now take me to your Leader.'

'He's a mouthy fucker,' one guard said to the other. And he laughed. 'OK, Mr Grant, you can go inside.'

Inside there was a male servant. I was shown through to a large room. Women did not appear to be much in evidence at the Molodi ranch. And whoever had chosen the quality furnishings had chosen a mix of styles. There were solid wood cabinets, tables and chairs, leather sofas and chairs, wicker and cane furniture and soft furnishings. Long curtains in purple colour kept out the heat of the day and protected the carpet and furniture from the direct sun.

The servant indicated a chair but with my back I preferred to stand.

I was kept waiting about ten minutes. Maybe the guy was busy; or maybe he was making a point.

Kaspar Molodi was a tall man, grossly overweight. He looked like pictures I'd seen of Chief Lobengula. Considering his bulk, he had tiny feet, encased in black shining shoes, and he was fast on his feet. He strode over and held out his hand in greeting.

'Thank you for agreeing to see me, Grant,' he said.

'Mr Grant,' I said.

He smiled. 'They said that you do not fear.'

'Is there anything I should fear, Mr......er?'

Again he smiled, and again he held out his hand. 'Kaspar Molodi.'

We shook hands and he signalled for me to sit down.

'What are you drinking, man? Beer?'

'Malawi rock shandy,' I said. 'And don't forget the bitters.'

He went to the door and gave orders to a servant.

He lowered his bulk into an easy chair.

'Cigarette? Cigar?' he suggested.

'Why am I here, Mr Molodi?'

Yes, you are British. You do not understand what it is that oils society.'

'Tell me why I'm here. Tell me that you know the name of my father's murderer. Then I'll be as sociable as hell.'

A servant entered, carrying a tray. He gave me my Malawi rock shandy – a beer glass packed with ice, with added soda, ginger ale, and a dash of Angostura bitters. Just the thing for a hot sticky day, although it was pleasant enough in that room, with the air conditioning working. The servant passed Molodi his beer. Molodi had elected to drink straight from the bottle, which glistened with cold. Only the British are daft enough to drink warm beer.

'I am the regional governor,' Molodi said, after taking a

good swig of his Castle lager. 'You come into my region and you make accusations. You put a stick into the clear water.'

'Do you, as regional governor, give orders to du Toit?'

Molodi smiled again. He smiled a lot. And the smile was totally false.

'The law took its course. It was agreed that your father committed suicide,' Molodi said.

Now it was my turn to smile, and my smile was totally false as well.

'My father blew the top of his head off. Right?'

'That is correct.'

'And then calmly reloaded and shot himself again. Is that what you're saying?'

Molodi drank more lager. He put down the bottle. And then patted his enormous belly.

There was what seemed a long silence. Molodi was waiting for me to continue. So I did.

'I've only been in Hopesfontein for a short time and already I've been told by just about everybody that I ought to get back to England, that my father killed himself, that he controlled black prostitutes. I have been accused of raping a tart and sodomising her. I've been made to dig my own grave and beaten with sjamboks.' I paused briefly. 'Welcome to South Africa. Welcome to the Rainbow Nation.'

Molodi smiled. It was a nervous smile.

'And now,' I continued, I'm in the ranch house of Kaspar Molodi, regional governor, ANC bigwig. Why do you need Israeli security guards, Molodi?'

'Mr Molodi,' he said.

We both laughed, out loud.

'I'm having another beer, man,' Kaspar Molodi said. 'What are you drinking this time, Grant?'

'Brandy,' I said. 'With ginger ale.'

Molodi did not move from his chair, but shouted for his servant. The guy must have been hanging about within earshot.

'Two beers for me. Brandy and ginger ale for my friend.'

He gave his orders in English.

Three beers already, and the sun was nowhere near the yardarm Little wonder this guy was grossly overweight.

'I have enemies,' Molodi said, his voice almost a whisper. 'I need people whose loyalty is to me alone.'

'Hence the Israelis.'

'But you are an Israeli,' Molodi said.

'No. I come from a Jewish family. I am British.'

'This area....they are not my tribe. I need security. And I also have business interests.'

'You've made enemies?'

''Too much,' he said.

This was no time to correct his use of English.

'What kind of business are you in, Kaspar?' I asked.

'Import and export,' he replied vaguely.

Now it was my time to smile. 'Import and export, eh? That covers an awful lot of sins,' Kaspar.'

'Let me explain to you, my friend. Then you will understand that my life is not easy. More brandy?'

I needed to keep my head clear so I declined. I didn't want an interruption. I had got this guy talking. About himself. Probably his favourite subject.

'Import and export, Kaspar.'

'Ag, yes. I am telling you, Mr Grant, there are many problems. Many problems.'

'But you, Kaspar – you're doing well. I congratulate you.'

I shook him warmly by the hand. He was well on the way to drunkenness now.

'So tell me! What do you know of my father's death?'

Kaspar laughed broadly.

Your father. Davy. He was a good man.'

'That's what everyone says. So how come he got himself murdered?'

'Yes,' Kaspar Molodi said, conspiratorially, 'Davy being killed. That was the badness.'

He leaned right over. His breath was foul with beer. He handed the bottle to me. I accepted it, not wishing to break the spell.

'Tell me, Kaspar. This is my family's honour.'

I took a swig of the beer.

Molodi gave me the name of my father's murderer.

ELEVEN

The bastards jumped me as I was walking to the hotel.

The streets were deserted. They were nowhere to be seen and then, suddenly, they'd jumped me, and one of them was holding a blade to my throat,

All the way back from the Molodi ranch I had been silent. The driver tried to talk to me at the start, but he soon gave up. I instructed him to drop me off about a couple of miles from the hotel. He told me that wasn't wise; there were tsotsis everywhere these days, and they would rob you for the clothes you were wearing. I insisted and he stopped the vehicle.

'Go well, Mr Grant,' the driver said.

'Stay well,' I mumbled in response.

After what Molodi had told me I needed to think, and walking helped me to think clearly. In the cool of the evening was a good time for walking.

In the old days towns were usually divided into three sections: white, African, and Indian. This applied to shopping areas and to housing. Especially to housing. I think I was walking, head down, not looking about me, in what had been an Indian zone. You have to remember that these people called Indians had, in most cases, never been to India. They had been brought over in the 18th and 19th centuries to work in the sugar cane fields after slavery was abolished in the British Empire. Some Indians were shipped to Fiji, Trinidad, Mauritius, and many to South Africa.

I wasn't thinking of this as I walked past the cloth shops and the general stores.

They were able to take me completely by surprise. One of them held me from behind and pressed the blade against my Adam's apple; if the bastard pressed any harder, he would surely raw blood, and it would be my blood. The second guy also held a knife but he stood in front of me, just far enough away to be sure I would not kick him in the balls. Both were hooded and scarves covered their faces.

'What you been doin', Grant?' the front guy said.

I could not speak. The slightest movement of my throat and the guy behind would have sliced into my larynx, the Adam's apple.

'You don' know what you fuckin' doin', Grant,' the talkative one said.

Apart from the fact that he seemed not to know about pronouncing the final 'g' in words, those two rasping comments made it obvious these guys were not whites, and were not Africans, either. That left only one racial group in Hopesfontein, unless these guys were some throwback to Hottentots.

I tried to lower my head, to push the larynx further back, but the guy behind me held on to my hair and pulled my head back, making sure my larynx was forward, the easier to cut with his blade.

The mouthy one had a message for me.

'Lissen to me, you Jew bastard! This time we goin' to let you go. But you better be leavin' this dorp pretty soon.' He paused, and it was not to search for the missing letter 'g'. 'You keep away from our family. Right?' He came close, his face about an inch from mine. 'Right, Jew bastard?'

Getting close, even gettin' close, was a mistake on his part. His proximity to me made his partner relax. I could feel the relaxation. The stupid twat was changing the blade from one hand to the other.

I did not wait. I brought up my right knee and caught the mouthy one in the cods. At the same time I deflected the knife blade, but not enough. He cut into my arm. I wanted to shake myself free from the moron behind. I made a slight movement forward. It was enough. He went sailing over my shoulder and landed on his pal. I do not know which of the three was most amazed. I think it was me. It had been a long time since I had actually thrown someone over my shoulder so easily, and with no effort.

I kicked the moron in the face. There was a crack. Probably a broken nose. Or if I were lucky, I'd smashed his jawbone. The jawbone of an ass. The mouthy one started to run. I went after him. At the school I attended the winter game was rugby union. I had never been chosen to represent the form, the house, or the school, and had no regrets. But I had watched the others playing and something must have been taken on board, for now as I came closer to the fleeing youth I dived and grabbed his ankles. He came down hard. I smashed my fist into his face. I tore off the scarf he had used to hide his features. Sure enough, his features were those of an Indian youth. I sat astride his chest and repeatedly punched his face. There was blood and snot flying everywhere, some of it on to me. I never even bothered to ask the little bastard if he had AIDS/HIV, which is a scourge in this country.

I stopped when I felt weary. I stood up. Gingerly, I felt at my throat. As far as I could tell, and with all the blood it was not easy, the moron had not cut into my larynx.

'On your fucking feet, Ali,' I said.

For the first time I felt pain in my right arm, where the knife had caught me. A closer examination would have to wait.

The mouthy guy was struggling to get to his feet. It wasn't easy; I'd given him a good pummelling.

I grabbed his arm and helped him to his feet. He was shaky. He stood there, unsteadily, his legs slightly splayed.

'What's your name?'

He did not answer.

In the Bible it says somewhere that a soft answer turns away wrath. There is another proverb: 'Kick them hard in the cods, and they see your point of view.' That is from the Lew Grant Encyclopaedia of Survival.

I kicked the guy in the cods. Hard, and I was wearing boots. He fell to the asphalt again., clutching his vitals. With any luck, I had terminated his reproductive years.

I knelt down beside him.

'Now....your fucking name,' I whispered.

'Mohammed Ali,' he uttered through his pain.

Why was I not surprised?

'Do you have any other name? A family name.'

'Daddah,' he said, and in those two small syllables was a mountain of pain.

'And tell me, Mo! Do you have a family member called Zohra?'

'She....she is my sister.'

'Is she then? Is she really?'

I looked around. The street was still empty. No cars had passed, everybody seemed to be snug in their houses, watching television, or perhaps in beer halls, seeking happiness in a bottle of beer.

'Just one more question, Mo,' I said.

I hoped he would object to my shortening of the prophet's name, but he lacked the energy, or perhaps the faith.

'Tell me. Am I a Jew bastard?'

He hesitated.

'No,' he said softly.

I stood up. The cut in my arm needed attention.

'I think you should be going home now, sonny,' I said. 'It must be well past your bedtime.'

I walked quickly down the street. I even passed the Hopesfontein HyperMart and wondered what the lovely Zohra was doing right now.

Within minutes I had reached the hotel. Elias Peteni was standing at the reception desk. He looked horrified. He handed over my room plastic without a single word, but his mouth was wide open.

'You should see the other fellow,' I said, and tried to laugh, but the pain was now too much for laughter.

Being tired, I decided to take the lift to the third floor. As I stepped out I saw a female figure in the corridor and was not surprised to see that the girl was outside my very door.

'Well, fuck me,' I said. 'You have got some neck.'

'I can explain,' she said.

'I think you had better.'

She followed me into the room and I made no attempt to keep her out. She was still wearing the school uniform. In fact, she looked quite fetching.

'Come into the bathroom, Chiko,' I said. 'You can bathe my arm.'

She smiled. Cheekily. No doubt she took me for a stupid white liberal.

I leaned against the sink in the bathroom.

'Listen, Chiko. I have just kicked shit out of a guy and if you speak one wrong word I do the same to you. Right?'

'Let me help you remove your clothes,' she said.

'Yes, that is something you're really good at, isn't it?'

TWELVE

I put my black shoulder bag on, went downstairs to reception, and out into the warm sunshine. I was, n certain ways, beginning to like being in Hopesfontein. What I particularly liked was the fact that just about anything I needed was within walking distance.

Outside the hotel, taxi drivers hovered like mosquitoes, anxious for a bite. With me, they were wasting their time. If I needed a car, I could always call Aggie's relative, young Freddie.

The library cannot have taken long to construct. It was a simple prefabricated building. On one side was a small hotel, with a bar and a small shop attached. On the other, a little further along, a secondary school, with a high fence all round – whether to keep thieves out or the kids in, I could not tell. There was sand all round the library building. One day, for sure, they would get round to covering the earth with asphalt, and it would be the poorer for it.

Since I'd last visited her Miss Ngulube had not improved. She did not smile as I entered. I had a distinct feeling that she believed the books were to be protected and loaned out only if it could not be avoided.

'Good morning, Mr Grant.'

'Good morning. You remember my name.'

'Every person in Hopesfontein knows your name, Mr Grant.'

'Famous, am I?'

I was trying to loosen her up, but she was not a woman for loosening.

'I need your help, Miss Ngulube,' I said.

She did not answer.

'Your assistance in finding out some important facts.'

'A library is for learning and for leisure,' she intoned, as if from a textbook, or perhaps an essay she had written while studying for the certificate in librarianship, or whatever these people get. 'We have a strong reference section.'

'Good. Where is the reference section, please?'

I noticed that everything had to be prised out of this young woman, question by question. She lacked initiative. Of course, if she'd had any initiative at all, she probably would not be rotting in a provincial library. She had the look of a virgin. It would take many questions to prise open her thighs. Not that I was interested in sexual activity or even sexual thoughts; Chiko had sucked me dry, in a manner of speaking, the previous evening, and had even bandaged my arm with material supplied by Elias Peteni. Why, I wondered, did he allow residents of the hotel to entertain guests in their rooms all night? Perhaps he would charge me for Chiko when I came to settle up.

Miss Ngulube led me to what was a small corner of the library. She found a red leather- backed book, thick and forbidding.

'This is for reference only, Mr Grant, and cannot be borrowed under any circumstances.'

That's what it said inside the book, too. Miss Ngulube was repeating another mantra. No doubt the repetition of these rules and regulations allowed her a measure of comfort and security in a system that she probably did not yet fully understand.

'Tell me, Miss Ngulube,' I said, 'what is the Dewey Decimal System?'

She did not even look surprised, did not wonder why I should ask her such a question.

'It is a system of library classification developed by Mr Dewey in 1876. It is used all over the world and not only here in South Africa.'

'You'll do for me, Miss Ngulube,' I said.

'Sir?'

'You are an intelligent young woman and the library service is lucky to have you as a librarian.'

She looked suitably modest and I could tell she was pleased.

Mrs van Niekerk had told me Miss Ngulube knew nothing, not even the Dewey Decimal System of library classification, and Mrs van Niekerk had been wrong.

'I think that you need the computer, Mr Grant,'she said.

My compliment had done the trick.

'Please come to the office.'

In the office there were two computer screens. At one a young girl was working.

'Doreen, you can be on the counter,' Miss Ngulube said imperiously.

The girl smiled. This was perhaps some sort of promotion. She bent over to pick up her handbag. I had a good view of generous tits.

They say that men think about sex every fifteen seconds. How do they manage to hold out for so long?

With the librarian's help I was soon into online reference. She insisted on remaining beside me, so there was no opportunity for privacy. I wanted to learn about the chain that owned the Hopesfontein Hotel. No problem. It was part of a para-statal holding company. This had been set up in 1995, not long after the transition to majority rule in South Africa.

'What happened to your arm, Mr Grant?'

She reached out an timidly touched the bandage that Chiko had applied the previous evening.

'I was walking back to the hotel and some bastard wanted to help me carry my money.'

I saw her wince.

'Forgive my bad language, Miss Ngulube.'

'It is Lina,' she said.

'What?'

'My first or Christian name. I am Pascalina.'

'Lew,' I said.

We shook hands demurely. She smiled. I realised that she was coming on to me. Even ugly women in narrow spectacles need love and affection, I suppose.

'Tell me, Lina.'

'Yes, Mr Lew?'

'Do you like food? Daft question. Would you like to go out with me for a meal one evening?'

'There is nothing here in Hopesfontein,' she said. 'But there is a place down the road - '

'I know the place. Gambling.'

'And much more, Sir. There is one very good restaurant, the Enchanted Forest.'

'Good! That's where we'll go. But first -'

'Your investigations. I can help you.'

Did I not mention that at the age of thirty-four, in good physical shape, able to think swiftly, with a ready wit, I am attractive to women?

I remained in the office until five o'clock, closing time. This seemed rather early. People who had a job would find it difficult to attend the library. Perhaps they all poured in on Saturday morning? Or they stayed at home to watch television.

I made notes. I am right-handed and with bandages on my arm it was not easy to write. Some things I pasted and copied. Lina Ngulube had no problem with me using the printer.

At five o'clock she let me and the young assistant out. We shook hands yet again and I said I'd be in touch. She took out her mobile telephone.

'I can give to you my cell number,' she said.

I told her that this was not necessary. I could always contact her at the library.

Within ten minutes, sweating a little, I reached the house where Sol Isaacs lived with Aggie.

He was sitting on his stoep. In his hand was a bottle of Castle. Did nobody ever use beer glasses in this dorp?

'What happened to your arm, young Lew?'

I told him, and what I'd done to the Indians who had waylaid me and threatened to cut my gizzard.

'Did I not warn you? Walking the streets after dark. I thought Davy's boy was bright but it seems he is a dumkopf.' He paused. 'You hurt them, you say?'

I had to repeat how I had slugged it out and had kicked Mohammed hard in the cods, and how he must still be in pain, assuming that his balls had not retreated into his body, in search of a place of greater safety.

'The knife is the weapon of choice for them young,' Sol said.

He took the top off a Castle and passed it to me. It was cold, straight from the fridge, and I drank deeply.

'You got a knife, Lew?'

'I have something better,' I said.

I showed him the Vector. He nodded approval and told me to put it away before a passer-by noticed. People were passing in the street, on their way home from work. Some greeted Sol and he responded briefly and courteously, but never once smiled.

Sol finished his beer and opened another two; he passed the second to me.

'So what did Kaspar want?' he asked.

I was surprised. 'How did you know -?'

'This is a small town,' Sol said. 'So for what did he want to see you?'

'I wasn't quite sure at first. All that treatment, being taken to his ranch in a Mercedes CrewBus.'

'Kaspar is not short of a rand or two,' Sol said softly.

It was the usual. For Hopesfontein, that is. Beer and talk.'

'How did you get the Vector past the guards?'

'Did you know they are Israelis?'

'Like I told you, Lew. This is a small town.'

I told him that I had not carried the gun on that occasion. If I had, I might well have shot Mohammed and his brother right there in the street, when they attacked me.

'So what did Kaspar want?' Sol asked, keen to get me back on track.

'To tell me who killed my father.'

Sol's face screwed up. Whatever name I was about to divulge, he was going to be dubious.

'Daddah,' I said. 'Old man Daddah.'

'And you believed him?'

I rubbed the palms of my hands together, and felt pain in my wound.

'There was no reason to doubt his word,' I said.

'No reason,' Sol, said with a sound that was half derisive laughter and half a snort. 'Except that Kaspar Molodi is a lying bastard, a clever politician, a drunkard, and ruthless in business.'

'Yes, Sol,' I said earnestly. 'I was in the library this afternoon. I learned a lot about Kaspar's business interests.'

Sol stood up. Held out his hand. 'Gaan dit reen? No, I do not think so. Come, Lew, let us go for a walk. Let us walk together down the street.'

Sol Isaacs was an old man and his movements were slow. As he walked, he occasionally clutched at his abdomen, as if he were suffering pain. It could have been excess acid in his stomach. I did not ask any questions. His breathing was stertorous.

Others were also sitting on their stoeps, in the cool of the early evening. Greetings were exchanged, in English and in Afrikaans. At the end of the road there was a small area that had been landscaped. There were three benches, all empty. Sol sat down heavily.

'So what did you learn in our municipal library?'

I sat down beside him.

'I learned that the hotel group which owns the hotel' – I did not need to specify which one - 'is owned by a consortium set up by the government. There are many

shareholders. But the two main shareholders are Mohammed Daddah – the old man – and our friend Kaspar Molodi. Kaspar has several blocks of shares, none in his own name, but all in the names of companies he controls.'

Sol took a deep breath.

'And if Kaspar can get his hands on Daddah's shares......'

'He'd be a serious rival to the Sun group,' I said. 'Hotels in all Africa and even some in the West Indies.'

'So Kaspar tells you that Daddah shot your Daddy. You kill Daddah. He pounces like a leopard on its prey.'

Sol Isaacs made a pouncing movement with his hands.

'I'm not exactly an idiot, Sol,' I said. 'Not a dumkopf.'

Sol smiled. It must have been my bad pronunciation.

So what are your plans?'

'I could report the allegation to du Toit.'

Sol snorted again.

'I could shoot Daddah for killing my father.'

'And go down for the rest of your natural. I have done time in these prisons. You would not survive.'

'You survived,' I said.

'That was in the old days,' Sol, replied. 'It will be different now.'

'Is there capital punishment?'

'Abolished in 1995,' Sol told me. 'And now we are the murder country of the world.'

'So,' I laughed, 'when I shoot Daddah, I won't be topped.'

'After six months in chokey, you will wish they had topped you, Lew.'

'So Molodi wants me to kill Daddah so he can take the shares. Therefore...'

'Therefore, what?'

'The killer of my father is Kaspar Molodi.'

Sol Isaacs looked at me directly. His eyes were watery and sad.

'Did they never teach you how to reason at university?' he asked.

'I never went to university,' I said.

He said nothing for a while. When he spoke it was quietly, earnestly, with the utmost gravity.

'Lew. This is a small town and the fastest and most reliable method of transmitting news is through gossip. And the gossip has been, these twelve months, that it was Kaspar or someone sent by Kaspar who killed your father, my friend David Grant. Shortly after the death, the holding company purchased the hotel. They have been buying all over the country. Your father had become unpopular because of the whores.'

I nodded my understanding but did not speak.

'Du Toit is in Kaspar's pocket, and he knows it. Nothing to be gained there. Daddah is a hard, tough businessman. Probably up to his ears in nefarious dealings of one sort and another. But he is not likely to be a killer.'

'Unlike his sons,' I muttered, feeling my right arm.

'They jumped you, son. But they did not kill you,' Sol said.

I nodded my agreement.

'Kaspar joined the struggle late. He could see the way the

wind was blowing. He had heard rumours that Mandela was about to be released. So he became very active in the ANC and spent a few weeks on Robben Island.'

'Long enough to be rewarded when the ANC came to power.' I said.

'Kaspar will stop at nothing, including murder. He is your man.'

'So I kill him,' I said.

'You'd never get past his security.'

'I got past today.'

'You were not armed, and you were almost surely being watched on internal television. What do they call it?'

'CCTV.'

'Ja! CCTV.'

'Don't worry, Sol. I will find a way. He killed my father and stole his living, and he will die.'

Sol shook his head sadly.

'Your blood is hot. Our cause is just. But you must not sacrifice your own life.'

'Not even for my father?'

'Not even your father,' Sol replied.

'There has to be vengeance,' I said. 'Justice must be done.'

'I think I know what has to be done,' Sol said.

'Then tell me,' I said.

'Patience, son. You are past thirty years and you have not yet learned patience.' He stood up. 'Let us walk back to the house.'

We went back along the road, nether of us speaking. When we reached Sol's stoep, Sol was breathing heavily. He shook my hand. It was clear that I was not being invited in.

'Come to see me tomorrow,' Sol said. 'At this time. I think I know the answer to your problem.'

'My problem is Kaspar Molodi,' I said fiercely.

'Tomorrow, at this time,' Sol said again, 'and discuss this

with no one. Goeie naand.'

'Good evening,' I replied.

We shook hands again. Suddenly the pain in my right arm seemed less, but the pain in my heart was heavy.

THIRTEEN

Chiko was not in the room. I checked to see what she had stolen but found nothing missing. The items important to me, passport for example, my money, were in the pack on my back. I never moved without that, especially when Chiko was sharing the room with me. A good shag she might be, but probably also not acquainted with the concept of private property.

I removed the bandage from my arm and then took a shower. The cut was still livid so I put the bandage back on. It was not easy; at such a time I needed Chiko, and she was absent from the room. With my arm uncovered, for I was wearing a short-sleeve shirt, I walked along to the bar. It was crowded and noisy. The drinkers were all men. No sign of Chiko. She claimed, in any case, to be a teetotaller and had gone to the bar only to dance. At the moment there was no music playing – all the noise came from loud conversation,and laughter, the signs that men have taken quite a number of beers.

I decided to let, as my mother used to say, fresh air get to my wound. My mother was wrong, of course: the air contains an army of bacteria and viruses, all of which would like to make a home in the cut in my right arm.

There were about ten people in the hotel restaurant. There appeared to be only one waiter on duty. I sat down at a table where I could see the verandah outside. Men and women were sitting on the verandah, drinking. Compared with the bar upstairs, it was all quiet and reserved.

'Good evening Mr Grant,' the waiter said.

'I'll take a Castle,' I said. 'Then I'll order. Where's the menu?'

'It is a buffet, Sir.'

'Sorry, what did you say your name was?'

'Ipileng,' the waiter said.

'Yes, Ipileng. Of course. Tell me, how long have you

worked here, Ipileng?'

'I am working here three years, Sir,' he replied.

'Good. Good. OK. So you fetch the Castle, in a glass, and I'll see what the buffet has to offer.'

What the buffet had to offer looked plentiful at first glance but closer inspection revealed three basic foods, potatoes, rice and pap. This last is a hard porridge made from mielie meal, or maize flower. By itself, it is tasteless and unappetising. It all depends on the accompanying relish. I put pap on my plate and surrounded it with mixed vegetables all cooked, and green and red chilis. This was going to be hot, so I also took some amasi, which is a thick sour milk, not unlike unsweetened natural yoghurt.

I ate slowly. I had no plans to go out again that evening. Ipileng brought my beer but no glass. I reminded him that I had asked for a beer glass. He was profuse in his apologies.

'Do you like working here, Ipileng?'

'It is a job, Sir.'

'Yes, but do you enjoy the work?'

'There are many people unemployed in South Africa,' he replied.

So I deduced that he did not particularly like working in the service industry but it was preferable to being out of work.

'What time do you knock off, Ipileng?'

'Sir?'

'At what time do you complete your work?'

'Ten o'clock.'

'Then what?'

'Sir?'

'Do you take a beer after work?'

'I do not take beer, Mr Grant.'

That was something I was beginning to learn about black Africans – they were either TT or drunkards. The middle way of social drinking, as far as I could tell from my short stay in Hopesfontein, was unknown.

I finished my meal. I had drunk two beers and eaten all the amasi, my way of dealing with the chili heat.

I went to the buffet to check the puddings. I chose a piece of jam roly-poly and poured warm custard over it. As I was eating, the waiter came to ask if I wanted coffee.

'You knew my father, David Grant, didn't you?'

'Yes, Sir.'

'Did you like working for him? Was he a good man?'

Ipileng looked around the restaurant. H rubbed his chin. There was no way I was going to get a straight answer.

'Come on, Ipileng! You can tell me. I will tell nobody else.'

'They killed him, Mr Grant.'

I kept my voice low.

'Who killed him, my friend?'

Again, he looked round, as if in fear.

'Tell me, Ipileng! Man to man! Who killed my father?'

'It is the spirits, Sir. The spirits.'

And he was off to another part of the room, fussing over diners. I never got my cup of coffee. But that did not matter, as I never drink coffee late at night.

On leaving the restaurant I was supposed to sign for the meal, and the cost would be added to my account. Ipileng avoided coming over, so I picked up a couple of Mint Imperials, good for sweetening the breath, and left without providing my signature. By the time I had walked up the stairs and along the corridor to my room I had crunched both mints and was wishing I'd grabbed a handful.

I unlocked the door and went in. And there she was, spread out on the bed. She was wearing her skirt and white top.

'Hello, Chiko,' I said, 'I didn't recognise you with your clothes on.'

There were tears on his cheeks. Tears from young women never impress me. They can turn the tap on and off at will.

'There is bad news,' she said.

I looked at her but did not speak.

'They say I must leave Hopesfontein.'

'So what's the bad news?'

'You will miss me,' she said.

'I shall miss shagging you, yes. But there will be others.'

'You do not love me.'

'No I do not,' I replied with emphasis.

'But I love you, Lew.'

'Fuck off.'

'Please take me to England.'

'I'm not sure my mother would approve,' I said. 'In any case, I do not love you.'

She sat on the edge of the bed and struck her fists together.

'Stop doing that,' I said to her sternly, 'and get your kit off. It's time for a shower.'

'There is no sex for you tonight,' she said. 'Because you do not love me.'

'OK, OK. But you are still going to take a shower.'

Once we were in bed – well, on the bed, in fact, lying on top of the sheet, both naked – I asked Chiko what Ipileng had meant, about the spirits.

She explained that many black Africans did not believe that death was a natural end to life. Any death must be the result of the work of the dark spirits. When a person died, even if they were old, the family members searched for a reason. Often, they consulted a witch doctor, a traditional shaman who claimed to understand the ways of witchcraft. He would generally explain that the death was the work of jealous neighbours. He would, for a price, seek to find the perpetrators, those who had consulted with the dark spirits and caused the death.

'Even some educated people believe these things,' Chiko said.

'And you?'

'I am a Christian,' she said.

'Yes, a Christian! You don't smoke. You don't take alcohol.'

'That is true.'

'But you shag like a rattlesnake,' I said.

She looked at my naked body. She smiled.

'Our friend, down there. I think he is awake now.'

'And raring to go,' I said.

I turned to grab hold of her, but let out a shout of pain.

'What is the matter, Lew?'

'My fucking arm,' I said.

Chiko reached over and kissed my wound.

I was touched by her action. But I still had no intention of taking her back with me to England. If I ever reached those shores again, that is.

'You must be gentle with me,' I said. 'I am a wounded soldier.'

She smiled and sat astride me. No sign of tears now. This is what she liked best, being on a bed with a man.

FOURTEEN

The supermarket was crowded. The owner was doing good business. Full trolleys were being pushed round. Noisy, recalcitrant kids making demands.

I bought a bar of chocolate. It was cold and hard. There were three check-out tills, all manned by young Indian females.

But no sign of Zohra Daddar.

There were long queues at each check-out. People stood patiently in line; there were no signs of tension that one finds in Britain, where people who have to wait quickly become impatient, and then abusive.

Eventually, I reached the front. I handed over my bar of chocolate.

'Where is Zohra?'I asked quietly.

The girl blushed and did not answer.

'I just want to greet her,' I said. 'I am leaving very soon.'

'She is in the back,' the girl said, afraid to give even that much information.

'The back?'

'The warehouse. It is out back.'

I moved on. At the door of the supermarket I unwrapped the chocolate. It was meant to be brown chocolate but it was almost white. I broke off two squares. Already they were starting to melt and leaving chocolate smeared on my hand. I put the squares in my mouth. They were tasteless.

There was a standpipe. I switched on and let the cool water clean my hand. I scooped water in the palm of my right hand and took a drink. Yes, I was taking a risk, but I had to clear the taste from my mouth.

Round the back there was a large roll door. It was fully open. Men driving fork-lift trucks were moving palettes about, like so many mosquitoes, except that mozzies come out after dark and these guys were wearing overalls and working in the heat of the sun.

Two large waggons were being unloaded. I did not bother to check what was being taken into the warehouse.

Nobody checked me as I approached the large open door and went inside, into the welcome shade. There was an office with large windows. Two men were sitting in the office, watching what was going on. I slipped quickly behind a pile of crates. Now I could not be observed by the Indians in the office. I just hoped they had not seen me enter. If they had, I might quickly find myself in deep shit. Metaphorically speaking.

I looked round as best I could, looking to catch sight of Zohra. I heard her voice before I saw her. She was giving directions to men driving the fork-lift trucks. Her instructions were quiet and polite, and yet strong.

Then I saw her. She was a vision of delight.

I called her name: 'Zohra!'

She looked round, anywhere but in my direction. I repeated her name. It came out almost like a hissing sound. Now she saw me but did not by movement or word betray that fact. Gradually, still giving orders, she moved closer to the stack of crates.

'You must get out of here,' she said.

'I must see you again,' I said.

She shook her head.

'I must talk to you, Zohra. Please.'

Please was not a word I used often with a woman, but this girl was special, and in no way a tart.

'Wait outside,' she said. 'Now.'

As quickly as I could, I waited outside, confident that Zohra would soon join me.

I had to wait about five minutes. Then a fork-lift truck came fast toward me. I thought I was going to be lifted up on those broad blades. The driver slammed on the brakes at the last minute. He came over to me.

'Miss Zohra, she say twelve o'clock by the new building.'

And he jumped back into his seat and returned to his work.

I had not eaten breakfast, being still replete from the evening before. I stopped at a bakery – that was the name, Hopesfontein Bakery – and purchased two scones. I was asked if I wanted butter on my scones and when I agreed they were split in two and butter liberally plastered on. I went into a bottle store and bought a bottle of water. Then I walked to the railway station, found a bench in the shade of the baobab tree, and sat down to eat the scones and drink the cool water, my breakfast.

I even bought a newspaper but soon realised I had wasted my money. I did not have any interest in the regional news and could not concentrate my thoughts on the crossword puzzle.

I checked the time. It was eleven o'clock. I noticed there were squads of police officer marching in the road. A beggar came up to me and asked for money. He had boozer written all over him.

'Two rand, boss,' he pleaded.

'Why all the police officers?' I asked.

'Today the new offices they are opening them,' he replied in halting English.

'The Party offices?'

'Yes. Five rand, boss, for a cup of tea.'

'Who is opening the offices? Tell me for ten rands.'

He told me and I gave him the tenner. Then he scurried away, not to find a tea shop, but in the direction of the bottle store.

I walked into the railway station. There was a door leading to the booking desk and then to the platform. There was a man in railway uniform.

I greeted him and he returned my greeting. That was necessary before I could ask my questions.

'It is hot today,' I said.

'It is always hot, Sir, except in winter.'

'And then it is cold,' I said.

'Yes, and then it is cold.'

'They are opening the new offices today,' I said.

'Yes.'

'What time?'

He checked his wrist watch. 'It is half past eleven, Sir.'

'No, what time is the ceremony to open the new Party offices?'

'Sixteen hours,'he replied. 'Four o'clock.'

'Will you be there?'

'No. Sir. I am doing duty here at the railway station.'

'Who is performing the opening ceremony? At four o'clock.'

'The governor.'

You mean......'

'Yes, Sir. Mr Kaspar Molodi.'

I ran all the way to the hotel. It was not far.

And by twelve, on the dot, wearing clean shorts and a fresh short-sleeve shirt, my hair brushed, I was waiting at the appointed place.

The new building was swarming with coppers and with some civilians. Security precautions were perhaps going to be tight later on bur for now nobody bothered me as I stood there, waiting, and nobody checked the car that purred to a stop beside me

FIFTEEN

Zohra looked like a million dollars but there was also a look of anxiety on her face – it showed around her mouth, her full and lovely lips.

'I only have one hour,' she said at last.

I did not answer.

She drove fast along an empty tarred road. Travel by car did not seem the norm in the Hopesfontein region. Or perhaps everyone in town was preparing for the official opening. Zohra had the air conditioning full on and I felt comfortable for the first time that day.

After about three miles, when we were well out into the country, with no signs of human habitation, Zohra left the road and moved along a dirt road. There were three large rocks ahead, rocks about four or five times the size of a man. Struggling for existence, covered in dust, were straggly trees, which kept close to the rocks and seemed to form a circle. I imagined men and women dancing magical routines round the rocks many thousands of years ago.

Zohra brought the car smoothly to a halt beneath the shelter of two trees. She had not searched for this spot' she'd known exactly where she was taking me. She switched off the engine and unfastened her seat belt.

'You have been here before, haven't you?' I said.

She did not answer, stared straight ahead.

'I want to explain a few things, Zohra,' I said.

I have long followed the rule 'Never apologise, never explain' when dealing with women. OK, I have never been able to keep the rule entirely but it has been a good rule of thumb. I have mostly applied it to tarts and to those chicks I don't really care about. Now it was different. I wanted to be soft and gentle, to take Zohra in my arms, to assure her, whisper sweet nonsense in her ears, stroke her black shining hair. Dead right! I had fallen in love.

'My brother is still in pain,' Zohra said at last.

'My arm isn't healed yet,' I said.

'You went to see the governor, didn't you?'

Truly, there were no secrets in Hopesfontein.

'Kaspar sent for me,' I said.

'Why should he do that?'

I leaned over and tried to kiss her. She moved her head away, and my lips brushed the lobe of her ear.

We had less than an hour together. The clock was ticking fast and furiously. I had no wish to talk about Kaspar Molodi.

'You don't want to know about these things, Zohra,' I said.

There was pleasure in just saying her name.

'My father does!' she blurted out.

I looked at her closely. Our eyes met and then she turned away. Her lips were tense.

'And I thought it was because you wanted to be with me,' I said bitterly.

'I do! But my father -'

'What does he want to know?'

'What passed between you and Mr Molodi.'

'We talked about my father's murder.'

'Oh!'

'It was a waste of time, except for one thing.'

I reached over and this time she did not move away. I kissed her cheek. She blushed.

'You are a very beautiful girl, Zohra,' I said, like any love-sick swain through all the ages.

'Girl?'

'Young woman,' I said.

She turned in her seat and looked at me.

'You've been in Hopesfontein for only a few days,' she said, 'and you have made an impression. Everybody knows your name.'

'They knew the name of Grant before,' I reminded her. 'My father, remember?'

I reached into my back pack for the bottle of water I'd purchased earlier. I offered it to Zohra, but she refused with a slight movement of her head. The water was warm but it was necessary to clear the dryness in my throat.

'And why,' I asked, 'should your father be interested in what I said to Kaspar Molodi?'

She shrugged her shoulders.

'As you say, I've stirred the waters a bit since I arrived.'

'You have spent time with a prostitute,' Zohra said with venom.

I smiled. She was jealous.

'That means nothing,' I said.

'You share a room at the hotel.'

'Not while I'm in jail,' I said.

Zohra did not smile.

'Let's go in the back seat,' I said.

'Why?'

I felt foolish. This was not something I often felt. I was unmanned by my passion for this lovely girl.

'Time is short but we may have time to make love,' I said.

I was besotted, even minding my language.

Zohra's face screwed up and for a moment she looked anything but beautiful.

'After you.....after you have slept with that black prostitute?'

'That was nothing,' I protested. 'I am a man. It was.......nothing.'

She made no move to open her door and get into the back seat. I did not pursue the matter. No way was I going to have my way with this young woman. In ordinary circumstances, I could have waited, but today was no ordinary day.

'This is going to be the last time I shall have a chance to talk to you, Zohra,' I said.

'You are leaving town?'

'Yes. Leaving today. And I don't want to waste these precious minutes arguing or talking about trivial things.'

'I must tell something to my father,' she said.

'To explain your being out here with me?'

She nodded, bit her lower lip.

'Then tell him the truth,' I said harshly.'I was picked up by Kaspar after being released from prison. He was almost drunk but perhaps not as drunk as he wanted me to believe. He provided me with the name of the man who murdered my father.'

'Who was that?'

Her voice was soft and, even with only three syllables, shaky.

A businessman who wanted to get control of my father's hotel. The name of this businessman was.....let me see? I think I can remember it....ah yes! It was Mohammed Daddah.'

I let that sink in. It did not sink but struck her like a fist.

'That is not true,' she spat, and reached over to strike me. Even with my wounded arm, I was able to take hold of her and prevent her hitting me. Again she tried to slap me. I smiled, held her close and kissed her on the lips. She did not respond. Nor did she try to bite me or spit in my face after the kiss. This was no movie. This was foolish life in a small dorp in the southern part of Africa.

'I hope you enjoyed that,' Zohra said.

'I'd have enjoyed it better if I'd had some sort of response.'

'He took you to his place, Mr Molodi, to tell you a lie?'

''He had a plan, my dear. He insisted that your father killed my father. So......this is the way some men think. I would seek revenge and kill your father.'

'But my father did not -'

'I know that, Zohra! I may be a fish out of water here, but I didn't leave all my brains back in England.'

There was no point, and no time either, in trying to explain the ramifications of hotel ownership. I any case, I did not think my father's murder was to do entirely with business ambitions. There was another element: my father ran black prostitutes, whores, and thus knew secrets that people wanted to be entirely certain were kept secret. Like ambitious young politicians!

.'My father is a good man.'

What girl would not say that of her father? Roman emperors frolicked with their children after ordering massacres, and Heinrich Himmler like nothing more after a hard day's work in the office than to go home and play Beethoven.

'It's Friday lunchtime. Shouldn't you be at the mosque?'

'Only men attend Friday prayers,' Zohra said. 'As you well know.'

'Tell me about your brothers. How did they know I'd be walking alone in the evening?'

'They learned you'd gone to Mr Molodi's place. They waited on the road. They followed you into town and saw you get out of the CrewBus and start walking. Are you going to report the attack?'

'To the police?' I sneered. 'But tell your dad to keep the buggers on a short leash.'

There was a short period of silence that seemed like an eternity. I glanced at the clock. It was fast coming up to one o'clock. I felt like a condemned man, waiting for the hour, the tolling of a bell, and the executioner's rope. There was a sinking feeling right in the pit of my abdomen. The nerves of my solar plexus, aware that with this beautiful girl, unlike so many others I had known, I was not going to get my end away.

I reached over and took hold of Zohra's hand. I kissed her fingers. I placed her hand down on my crotch area. She quickly withdrew and again she was blushing deeply.

'Start the engine,' I said wearily.

Zohra drove the car back to town. Neither of us spoke a single word. She dropped me where she had picked me up, by the new office block.

I got out of the car, closed the door behind me without saying anything, and she drove away to her family and her prison.

The finishing touches were being made to a stage. It looked like a place for executions. There were the steps. There would be the axeman's block. A police brass band was practising. I don't know much about playing music but even a deaf ear like mine could tell the guys were not playing well.

I asked a young cop what time the ceremony started. He told me four o'clock. I think I had known that already.

I walked to the Hopesfontein Palace Hotel, which until one year ago had been the Grant Hotel. I smiled at the thought. If I had arrived one year or so earlier, I'd have been able to meet the old man, and I'd have had the pick of his whores.

Elias Peteni was sitting on a chair in the reception area. Dorcas was behind the counter, sitting on a stool, pretending to be busy, but in fact only shuffling pieces of paper.

As I entered, Elias Peteni made an effort to stand up. I told him to remain seated, telling him he looked tired and should rest. He sank back gratefully into his afternoon torpor.

I took the door pass key and ran up the three flights of stairs. There was the noise of men in the public bar.

I opened the door. I had decided that I would shag Chiko, grab a couple of hours sleep, and then walk down to observe the celebrations. But Chiko was not there and there was no sign of any of her clothing.

I pulled back the mattress. The Vector was where I had hidden it. I weighed it in my hand. It felt right. I pushed the slide fully forward and cocked the hammer. I took the thumb safety off and held the pistol in its normal firing grip. I pulled the trigger and the hammer fell. I did it again. On the bedside locker, there was a pencil and a ball point pen, next to writing paper. I inserted the pencil into the barrel, eraser end first. I pulled the trigger and the pencil was propelled out of the barrel with some considerable force. The next and last task was to load the pistol with ammunition.

SIXTEEN

After two hours of sleep I felt fully refreshed. I shaved, took a shower and put on the safari suit, ideal wear for the hot weather, and with the added benefit of deep hip pockets. My arm was beginning to heal and I could use it more without feeling much pain.

I slung my back pack on, shut the room door behind me, and walked along the corridor. And down the three flights of stairs, without bothering to check if Chiko were in the bar. Chances were, I'd never see that tart again. I had the powerful feeling that I was doing things for the last time, as if I were moving to a different school, another town, or emigrating to another country. That last was correct – I was embarking on a journey from which no traveller returns.

Elias Peteni was behind the reception desk.

'Are you going t the ceremony, Elias?' I asked.

He shook his head dolefully.

'Dorcas will be there. It is her afternoon off duty.'

'See you later,' I said breezily, not expecting to see him later.

'Go well,' Elias said.

For time, I was cutting it short. But there was no need to hurry. This is Africa, and here nothing ever begins punctually.

As a spectacle it did not have much to commend it. But, then, this was a small town, not London, Paris or New York, where they know, from centuries of experience, how to put on a show.

The small stage was now ready. It had been hastily cobbled together. Lots of nails and big hammers, no dovetail joints. It was rough wood, which was right; after the opening ceremony it would become firewood at someone's house. Bunting had been arranged round the stage. There were two republic flags, hanging loosely in the torpid air.

The police were much in evidence. The band, now done up in their best gear, sought shade near the new building. There was a good turn-out. White tee-shorts were much in evidence among the younger members of the crowd. Little children held small flags. Everyone in that crowd was a black African. No Indians, I noticed. No white people, myself excepted. I felt like a bottle of milk in a sea of Castle lager, and not for the first time.

'Good afternoon, Mr Lew Grant.'

A man's voice behind me. I turned. Enoch Molloi stood there, his hand out in greeting. I shook the doctor's hand.

'Good afternoon, Doc. Can they spare you down at the hospital?'

'The dead are never in a hurry,' he said.

'Did you ever deal with the living?' I asked him.

'I still do,' he said. 'I have private patients. I make home visits.'

'There is a cost for this service, I suppose.'

'Oh yes!' Molloi laughed. 'Only whites and rich Indians can afford me.'

'What about pro bono work for poor blacks?'

Molloi pursed his lips. 'No, I never work for free.' He paused and then said, seriously, 'Here comes one of my private patients right now.'

Sol Isaacs should not have been out in that hot afternoon sun. He walked slowly and with obvious difficulty, and was holding a walking stick. If Sol saw me and Doctor Molloi, he did not acknowledge us. A black woman took hold of Sol's arm and led him to a chair near the platform.

'He doesn't look too good,' I said.

'He is dying,' Enoch Molloi said softly.

I shrugged. 'He's an old man. He's witnessed a lot of tragedy.'

'It might have been the shock of going to prison that triggered it.'

'Triggered what?' I said.

'His cancer. Did you not know he has terminal cancer?'

Enoch Molloi clearly did not hold much stock with such matters as a patient's privacy.

There was a flurry of movement behind the stage. Something was at last going to happen.

The band stood up and got into some kind of formation. I could see the sweat on all their faces and they had yet to start playing. Poor buggers, I thought. Join the police service and die of heat exhaustion.

The band started to play. People came to attention. I noticed that Sol Isaacs made an attempt to stand. It was a ragged performance. Small children knew the words; probably sang them every morning in school.

A number of men and women came up the steps to the stage. There were about eight of them. One man was an Indian.

The music finished, I turned to speak to Enoch Molloi.

'Let us live and strive for freedom, In South Africa our land.' he said, and it was clear from his voice that he did not care a damn.

'The National Anthem?' I said.

'Nkosi Sikelei Afrika,' Molloi said, smiling. 'God Bless Africa.'

'That man on the stage. The Indian -'

'Mohammed Daddah,' Molloi interrupted. 'Businessman, involved in charitable work, and pays a lot of money into Party funds.'

'Which he offsets against tax,' I said.

'Don't they all,' the Doctor shrugged.

'One of your patients?'

'Yes, but he's in good health.' He laughed. 'I also attend his family. Young Mohammed has been to consult me.'

'Crushed bollocks?'

'What did you use? Two hot bricks?'

Chairs, which ought to have been there before, were now being hastily passed up to the stage. There was barely enough room for eight chairs.

The band struck up again. It was show time. The main attraction. Top of the bill. Except that nobody showed.

'He's late,' I said.

'Perhaps they are trying to make him sober,' Doctor Molloi said with a careless laugh.

'Another of your esteemed patients, no doubt.'

Molloi did not deny it.

I felt a tug on my right arm. Too near my wound for comfort.

'Please come with me, Mr Grant,' a young man said. He was wearing spectacles, photochromic, and the lenses had blackened with the sun.

'Why should I?'

'Please, Mr Grant. We do not wish for trouble in a public place.'

'Who the fuck are you?'

He took out a card, and flashed it. Too quickly for me to see what it was but it certainly looked official.

'Police?'

'This will not take long, Mr Grant, and then you can return to the ceremony.'

We did not walk far, but far enough to find some welcome shade and be well away from the crowd.

'Hold up your arms, Mr Grant.'

'Are you really a policeman?'

'Yes. Hold up your arms, please.'

I'd never known cops to be so polite.

I held up my arms and the young man quickly took the Vector from the right pocket of my light suit.

'I think you will be safer without that, Mr Grant.'

I waited for the charge. Illegal possession of a handgun. Possession of a handgun with intent to endanger life. Specifically the life of a fat bastard who had no morals, political or otherwise. There was nothing.

'What now? I asked hoarsely, my throat suddenly dry.

The young man smiled. 'Well, Mr Grant, you can lower your arms.'

'And next?'

'Join the crowd. Enjoy the opening ceremony.'

'How did you know?' I asked.

'Let us say – something that my mother told me when I was a young boy – let us say that a little bird informed me.'

'My mother used to say the same thing. Maybe all mothers do.'

'Oh yes, Sir, there is one thing.'

The cop reached in his inside pocket.

'One railway ticket, Mr Grant. Hopesfontein to Jo'burg. Single.'

I refused to accept the ticket.

'Sorry, but there's unfinished business.'

I walked back to my place. Dr Molloi was no longer there. I saw him over the far side, close to Sol Isaacs. I took a long swig from the water bottle in my back pack, the water still warm. That was something I'd forgotten to do, before leaving the hotel. Well you cannot remember everything, not when you are planning to commit an act of political assassination, which is certain to end with your own body writhing on the hot ground, filled with lead from police handguns.

Although I had not been dead, I felt like a man who has been restored to life. There must, I decided, be other ways than using a gun.

The band struck up again. The National Anthem again. This time, to cheers and applause, Kaspar Molodi stepped out on to the sage. He was helped by two burly black guards. No sign on the Israelis; they were not for public notice. The guards stood one on either side of Molodi, perhaps to make sure he did not fall down.

He made a speech. It started off quietly enough. He was pleased to have been asked to open this grand new building. The contractors had done a good job. The office was needed by Party staff, not for their own convenience, but so that they could better assist the people, the ordinary voters. This was what the revolution had been about, why Nelson Mandela and his friends had conducted a struggle over any years. This was why he, Kaspar Molodi, although still a young man, had worked side by side with Nelson on Robben Island, breaking stones. So that the people might be free from the Boer oppressors.

And so he continued. What had started quietly and in a spirit of gratitude and conciliation now became a speech whose words were wrapped in hatred and venom. Kaspar Molodi had been captured by his own rhetoric.

Very quickly I stopped listening. I looked over to where Sol Isaacs was sitting, the sole white man in that crowd, apart from me, and I was a stranger in a strange land. Dr Molloi was nowhere to be seen. Perhaps he'd had the good sense to find shade and comfort in a beer hall. In such heat, beer made better sense than political rant.

As I scanned the crowd, I foolishly hoped to catch sight of Zohra Daddah. She might have accompanied her father, I thought. No such luck, Grant, you silly bugger. My eyes returned to Sol Isaacs. He should not have been there, in the sun, in that crowd, listening to this nonsense from the fat man sweating gallons up there on the stage. Sol should have been sitting on his stoep, living out his last days at home.

I saw him stand up. I thought he was going to turn and go in the direction of his home. Instead he stumbled toward the stage. Th two guards were suddenly alert but when they saw it was a frail old white man, they relaxed.

Sol reached the stage.

Kaspar Molodi looked down. Venom had disappeared. There was on his flabby soaked face a smile of benevolence.

Careful to speak into the microphone, Kaspar said, 'Sol Isaacs. My old friend. This man also suffered for the revolution. This man served his time in a Boer prison.'

He gave orders to his guards, off mic. They both jumped down and assisted Sol round to the steps and on to the stage. Sol Isaacs stood next to Kaspar. They shook hands. The crowd cheered. The dignitaries on the stage clapped dutifully.

Sol's hand was in his pocket. And suddenly there was a gun. He fired two shots into Kaspar's chest, one directly into the fat man's heart.

The cheering of the crowd turned immediately to screams, but they could hardly be heard for the hail of police bullets that hit the body of Sol Isaacs.

Back at the hotel, having slept undisturbed for about twelve hours, I ate lunch in the restaurant and then at about four o'clock in the afternoon settled my account. I was surprised that I had not been charged for Chiko'ss stay. I did not argue.

Elias Peteni shook my hand solemnly.

'It was a bad business yesterday, Mr Grant.'

'A very bad business, Mr Peteni,' I said.

'There is one thing, Sir.'

I was ready to be asked for something toward the cost of

Chiko's stay.

He took an envelope and gave it to me. I opened it. Inside was a railway ticket from Hopesfontein to Johannesburg, one way. I already had a return ticket and almost gave this one to Elias, but instead I put it in my black bag.

'The train comes at five o'clock.'

'It is always late,' Elias Peteni said. 'Go well, Mr Grant.'

'Stay well, Mr Peteni.'

The train was well and truly late, arriving at seven o'clock or thereabouts. It stayed on the station for a good half hour. I found a window seat in what was, I hoped, going to be a quiet carriage.

I looked out of the window at the melee on the platform. Which was not a platform at all. Then I saw Chiko, still dressed in skirt and white top but looking anything like a child. She was searching the carriages. I had no doubt of the person she was seeking. News travels fast in a small dorp like Hopesfontein.

I opened the window, It was one of the old sash kind.

'Chiko!'

She heard my voice.

'I will come with you,' she shouted.

'Do you have a ticket?'

She shook her head glumly.

'Buy one for me, Lew.'

'I have one here,' I said. 'I got it for you.'

She climbed in through the window. I had to assist her. She fell into my arms.

We were still the only two people in the carriage. If it stayed like that we should be able to shag several times before we finally reached Johannesburg the following day.

THE END

Ashgrove Crime

Ashgrove Crime invites authors to offer crime novels written according to the following guidelines:

- 30 000 to 40, 000 words.
- The story may be set in any part of the world.
- The story is told in the first or third person.
- The main plot tells how the protagonist, the hero, fights against the forces of evil within a particular society.
- Avoid sub-plots.
- Have a linear narrative – avoid flashbacks unless they are absolutely necessary.
- Build tensions – the forces or circumstances that prevent the hero achieving a quick resolution
- Achieve a satisfactory conclusion where the hero finally triumphs.

Be realistic. Set the story in a particular milieu. Contemporary settings are usually best.

Think Dashiell Hammett, James M. Cain, Raymond Chandler, the Black Mask authors, Hank Jansen, Mickey Spillane, Robert B. Parker – or any other successful crime writer of the past or present. But be sure the style and the story are your own.

Scenes of violence are acceptable if within the plot and/or the characters. The same with scenes of graphic sex. Think carefully before these are added to your story.

Ashgrove Romance

Ashgrove Romance would like to invite authors to offer romance novels written according to the following guidelines:

- 30 000 to 40, 000 words.
- Think Harlequin/Mills & Boon.
- The story may be set in any part of the world.
- The story is told from the main female character's perspective.
- The story is told in the first or third person.

The **heroine** may be from any national or ethnic background; should experience personal growth and self-discovery; realise her own worth and inner strengths.

The **hero** is strong and may be successful in his chosen field. Is attractive to women.

The plot

- The main plot-line revolves around the heroine & hero's struggle to build a romantic relationship.
- outside forces (at work or in their communities) try to keep them apart.
- their own conflicting beliefs about modern society and the role of women also threaten the development of romance.
- Avoid sub-plots
- Have a linear narrative – avoid flashbacks unless they are absolutely necessary.

- Build tensions – the forces or circumstances or beliefs that keep hero and heroine apart.
- Achieve a satisfactory conclusion where love finally triumphs.
- Intimate scenes may be included but avoid the most explicit kind of graphic sexual detail that may alienate some readers of this genre.
- Remember your target readership: the many readers across the English-speaking world who enjoy Harlequin/Mills & Boons books

Age groups: from teenagers to 65+, mainly but not entirely female.

Ashgrove Education

We welcome synopses or ideas for books on educational subjects.

Our intention is to build a body of work that will actually make a difference within this important field.

Your submission may be within any field of education, including textbooks for the primary, secondary and tertiary levels.

We are not prescriptive about length or form but we ask you to remember that the length and form must be appropriate to the age and interests of the end users, whether youngsters or adults.

Texts suitable for teachers in training are also welcome. Or for teachers already qualified who may be seeking fresh ideas and texts that have common sense allied to vitality.

Send an outline of your idea as an email attachment to info@ashgrovehousepublishing.com. Please insert EDUCATION in the subject box.